The Circle of Olympians

The Circle of Olympians

Sonya Haramis, M. Ed.

Edited by Joanna Paxinou

Published by

Peace of the Dreamer

Peace of the Dreamer
www.peaceofthedreamer.com

Copyright © 2006 by Sonya Haramis, M.Ed.
Copyright © 2004 by Sonya Haramis, M.Ed.
First Edition 2006

All rights reserved. No part of this book may be reproduced or transmitted in any form or by any means, electronic or mechanical, including photocopying, recording, or by any method not yet invented, or by any information, storage and retrieval system, without permission in writing from the author.

Disclaimer:
This story is fictional. Names, characters, places, and incidents are the product of the author's imagination or are used fictionally. Any similarity to persons living or dead, business establishments, events or locales is purely coincidental.

Library of Congress Control Number: 2005908190

ISBN: 0-9762247-1-2

Printed in the United States of America

For Joanna
Guardian Angel
Warrior of Faith

Acknowledgements

I would like to thank those who have taught me and protected me my entire life. I thank my beautiful teachers who have graced my path and lit the way, and those who never ceased to remind me of the magic within life.

And I would like to honor my Greek heritage by humbly offering this book. I am grateful for my Greek Orthodox faith, my training in the martial arts, especially at Aikido of Monterey, and the communion with Spirit that has always been with me.

A special thank you to Joanna Paxinou for her patience, support, enthusiasm, and her extraordinary editing.

I would also like to thank my circle of family and friends who always supported me through this and many other projects. Thank you all for being my Circle of Olympians!

Table of Contents

Chapter One: *Journey Within* 11
Chapter Two: *Morning Coffee* 17
Chapter Three: *The Amulet* 19
Chapter Four: *Destiny* .22
Chapter Five: *Quest* 25
Chapter Six: *Gaea* 28
Chapter Seven: *Reunion* 31
Chapter Eight: *The Ancient Ones Take Form* 34
Chapter Nine: *Herakles* 38
Chapter Ten: *Zeus* 41
Chapter Eleven: *Amphitrite* 46
Chapter Twelve: *Destined Journey* 56
Chapter Thirteen: *Artemis* 61
Chapter Fourteen: *Eos* .69
Chapter Fifteen: *The Sacred Grove* 72
Chapter Sixteen: *Enemy Revealed* 78
Chapter Seventeen: *Victorious Vow* 85
Chapter Eighteen: *Journey to Delos* 88
Chapter Nineteen: *Apollo* 93
Chapter Twenty: *Battle with Medusa* 104
Chapter Twenty One: *The Final Chapter* 116
Chapter Twenty Two: *Yia Yia* 122
Chapter Twenty Three: *Goodbyes* 125
Chapter Twenty Four: *Return to Ithaca* 131
Chapter Twenty Five: *The Aritifacts of Athens* . . .133
Chapter Twenty Six: *Return to California* 138
Chapter Twenty Seven: *Family Reunion* 142
Chapter Twenty Eight: *Joyous Revelation* 145

Chapter One

Journey Within

The wind caressed my face, hair, and being, greeting me at the threshold to Ithaca, Greece. Sailing into her mighty yet hidden harbor, so many thoughts raced through my mind. What awaited me here? What secrets would I learn the answers to? Would my heart ever mend? These questions poured through my heart as I anxiously waited to see my grandmother, my protector and devoted guardian. How wonderful it would be to see her again, and visit my sanctuary, one of the few things in my life that remained the same.

It had been some time since my last visit to Ithaca, and so much had changed in my life. I had grown up, but with that growth came so much loss. I felt as if I weren't whole anymore, having just lost my father and paternal grandmother, or Yia Yia in Greek. Just before those deaths, I ended my engagement and didn't know who I was.

As I was beginning to heal from my profound grief, I was laid off from my writing job with a telecommunications company in California. So many times in my life I had felt broken, and my grandmother, Euterpe, was there each time to pick me up, encourage me, and tell me I would do great things in my life. How blessed I was to still have her in my life, and to be on my way to her home in Ithaca.

The sun was barely rising. The dew and clouds still hung in the air, giving a small piece of heaven to remember throughout the day. Everyone aboard the boat began rustling, gathering bags, bits, friends, and children. I composed myself and gathered my two bags, stuffed with as much as I could fit, with small gifts for my grandmother and Uncle George (her brother who lived with her), and gifts for distant cousins.

Tears suddenly filled my eyes as I anticipated the tears she and I would shed together, for my losses were her losses, too. As those ahead of me and behind me pushed and shoved their way off the boat, I waited to let the crowd pass. I didn't want their haste to ruin my first moment and embrace with my grandmother. I searched the waiting crowd for her beautiful and powerful face. Somewhere in the midst of all those people stood a part of me, my grandmother.

There! I finally found her in the crowd of waiting people! I tried to catch her attention with my wave. She didn't see me right away, so I focused my attention and my love on her with my eyes. In an instant, she received my energy and found my gaze. Excitedly she waved back at me, tears streaming down her face. She started running toward the belly of the boat to get closer to the disembarking passengers. Even though she was old, no one dared push her around. The crowd seemed to part for her, not only because of her age, but because of her power. I wonder if they knew how strong she truly was?

The crowd within the boat dissipated, so it was time to get off and pass through the threshold into my new life, the life my grandmother would lead me towards. I made my way down the stairs, struggling with my bags, trying to keep my appearance presentable, and trying not to trip from my fast walk that was quickly becoming a run. Finally, I was at the lowest level and could see the horizon. As I walked

The Circle of Olympians

down the ramp to the dock, my grandmother opened her arms and her heart to me. I dropped my bags and embraced her with all of my being. All the pain I had felt, all the loneliness and grief evaporated in her arms. Everything I felt, she had survived. She had a look in her eyes that said, "Calliope, everything is going to be all right. Trust me." And I did.

But something was different about my grandmother this time. There was a different look in her eyes, and something about her energy was different. Or had my energy and awareness changed, better able to grasp who she truly was?

Uncle George was also there to help me with my bags and to escort us home. Seeing him made me feel as if everything truly would be all right. My great uncle and I embraced for a long time. He was never a man of many words, but he didn't need many to express his love for us. The love in his heart filled any room he was in, and I always felt safe being in his presence. As children, my cousins and I often wondered if he was Santa Claus, and to this day I still wonder.

With my bags gathered and my grandmother, Uncle George, and I interlocked in each other's arms, we walked to our ancestral home not far from the port of Vathi. Walking upon the uneven cobblestone pathway home, I felt as if I was walking through a threshold between the modern world and the ancient world, between the old me and the new me, and between what was known and what was unknown. I knew a great adventure was ahead of me. I didn't know which direction it would take me, but I knew I would be well protected by my grandmother.

Up a few hills, down a winding dirt path, we walked until we arrived at my grandmother's house, our ancestral home. Just seeing this place again made me feel safe. It was one of the only places that remained the same in my life, one of the few constants that was always ready to embrace me in its warmth and love. So many memories lived within the walls of this small, white washed home. I don't know how my grandmother kept so many memories alive, yet lived in the present moment at the same time. Because she was so alive, she was eternally young yet ancient at the same time, and she held great wisdom.

Uncle George followed behind us as we walked up the few steps to the front door. As my grandmother opened the front door, the aromas that filled the house filled my senses because she had cooked all week for me. The fragrance overcame my soul and healed its empty places with love. The smell of food, cooked by generations of my family and my elders, swept away my grief, for in that moment everyone I had lost was with me through the aromas of Greek food and through my grandmother. How was my grandmother able to do this? I was sure she had her own brand of magic that she used when she cooked.

My grandmother ushered me into my room, which had remained the same since my last visit. As I was her only granddaughter, I received special treatment from our family matriarch. She told me to get comfortable, change my clothes, and to let her and Uncle George take care of everything.

I could not express my joy at being there and being with her. I felt like a little girl again. Everything was all right. No one judged me or held me up to impossible standards. There, I was unconditionally loved, which was exactly what I needed that summer.

In the corner of my bedroom was a lit red candle in front of an icon of Jesus. On the simple, wooden nightstand by my bed was an icon of the Virgin Mary. I felt like they were old friends welcoming me home. I lay on the bed and closed my eyes, remembering times I spent there as a child when all the family members were alive and together. Life was always so easy at my grandmother's home, but I knew that was because of her constant love and strength. I wondered where she got that strength from, but looking at the icons in my bedroom, I knew.

My prayers of thanks were long overdue, and I knelt before the icon by my bed and gave thanks for my safe journey. Hiding deep within my soul, my grief reared its head for a moment and I felt profound sadness. I prayed to be free of this sorrow, and to find my true purpose in life, as I felt completely lost and had no idea where my life was going.

A strange, floral aroma suddenly filled the room, and for a moment I thought it was my grandmother's cooking, but it lingered long enough for me to know that it was not food, but an aroma from another world. I looked around and was aware of a deep silence that filled the room. I felt safe yet unnerved. Something unusual was happening, as if the aroma I smelled was telling me my prayers had been answered.

I looked at the icon of Jesus and it glowed in a different way than when I first entered the room. I closed the curtains at the window and walked closer to the icon to prove I wasn't crazy. Staring at the icon, directly in front of it, I witnessed that it was lit from within. His glowing Spirit was there, letting me know He was with me. I sobbed, and felt my grief leave me. This summer in my grandmother's home in Ithaca would be unlike any other. At last, some of the mysteries I had sensed about my grandmother all my life might be revealed to me.

Somewhere in one of my suitcases I had packed my journal to write down and remember every moment of that summer with my grandmother in Greece. I always loved writing, and wondered if it was because I was named after Calliope, the Greek muse of epic poetry.

I prayed to be inspired by the legends and miracles that land held, but was surprised that one of them was held in my grandmother's house. That summer I wrote about my feelings, what I sensed, how I felt, what I smelled. I wrote about the prayer I just prayed, and remained aware and present to the still unfolding mystery. I was thrilled and felt alive, something I had not felt in many years.

My grandmother called out to me, asking if I needed anything, and then came to my room. Even though I was an adult, she would never think of me as anything but her baby granddaughter. Nothing could have comforted me more. She came into the room and we sat on the bed, holding hands. Although I was exhausted, the only thing I wanted to do was hold her hand and feel like a child again.

Chapter Two

Morning Coffee

I slept peacefully my first night in Ithaca. The following morning, I joined my grandmother and Uncle George in the kitchen for breakfast and coffee. We always talked for hours over coffee whenever we visited with one another, a comforting ritual I would never be without. She made fresh Greek butter cookies, or koulourakia, that morning, and we dipped them into our coffee as we talked about everything. In no time at all, I was caught up with the local gossip.

Then the expected tears came, and we cried together, mourning the family we had lost. Even now, months and years after the deaths of loved ones, it didn't seem real. I kept expecting to see them... as if they had been away on holiday for an extended period of time. Even though they were gone, somehow and somewhere, I knew they lived, beyond time and beyond my conscious comprehension. My grandmother must have known this too, because her grief wasn't all consuming as I expected it to be.

Sipping coffee together, studying my grandmother's face, there was a look in her eyes that conveyed she had seen other worlds. I'm not sure I saw that glimmer before, but that didn't mean it wasn't always there. Perhaps I was the one unable to see the magic before grief opened the divine portal for me.

"I want to show you something," my grandmother said, sitting at the kitchen table.

She stood up and walked over to the kitchen cupboard, stocked with years' worth of recipes and secret ingredients. Behind many spice jars and copper pots, she took out a small, ancient jar covered with a wooden lid. Looking around the kitchen, to make sure no one but she and I were listening, she took out a ruby amulet and an ancient scroll of paper. Her eyes lit up when she held these things in her hands. I saw the same glow emanating from her as I had witnessed with the icons. I watched her hands closely, and felt something stir deep within my soul. Somehow these things looked familiar to me, as if I had once known them. She looked at me, half expecting me to recognize what she held in her hands. I looked at her, as if I was remembering part of a dream I had just awakened from.

"What I am about to share with you is sacred, secret, and meant for your ears only," my grandmother said softly. "You must swear to keep secret what I am about to tell you. It is absolutely vital you swear this. So much more is at stake than you are aware of. You are not yet completely aware of who you are and what you are to do in this life. Do you promise you will not betray me? You are my only granddaughter, the only person I can trust with what I am about to tell you."

"Of course, grandmother, I swear. You know whatever you tell me I will keep secret, whatever you ask of me I will do," I promised.

She came back to the kitchen table, holding the amulet and the scroll, and sat down beside me. She took a sip of her coffee as if to brace herself for what she was about to tell me. I watched her every move, knowing from deep within my being that what she was about to tell me would change my entire life.

Chapter Three

The Amulet

My grandmother was silent for a moment, sipping the last drops of her coffee, and contemplating what she was about to tell me.

"What is it? What does this mean? Who gave this to you?" I asked my grandmother. "I vaguely remember you showed this to me when I was a little girl, but I forgot about it until now."

She held her breath for a moment, as if gathering the energy she would need to reveal one of her most sanctified secrets.

She began, "When I was a little girl, my mother, your great-grandmother, told me a fantastic story every night before she sang me to sleep. I was mesmerized every night by her tale about a ruby amulet and a prized scroll, which revealed the secrets of the amulet and how to unlock its magic. I had dreams about this amulet. I knew one day I would discover how to use its magic to protect my mother and family.

"Calliope, when I was a little girl, there were horrible wars. I was afraid every night I went to bed. My mother tried to calm my fears with her stories and her cooking, but inside I was still afraid. Then one day she showed me this amulet I now hold in my hands. When I first laid my eyes upon it, I couldn't believe it.

"My mother was magical, and I thought she had it specially made for me so that I would believe the story she told me was true, but the amulet was and is real. She told me to hold the amulet in my hands and tell her what I saw and felt. At first I felt nothing, but then a warm glow radiated from the stone and its warmth traveled all the way up my arms to my heart, through my entire body. I felt my third eye open and I had my first vision of things I wasn't able to speak of for many years. My mother knew I had a vision, and watched me for my reaction. Our eyes locked and I knew she knew what I had seen. It was a silent initiation, which I am about to share with you now, but not in words."

My grandmother then placed the ruby amulet in my hands and told me to sit silently with it until I felt something. Immediately, I felt its warmth travel up my arms, just as it had when my grandmother first held it as a little girl. Its heat moved through my body, into and around my heart, and awakened my chakras. I felt on fire and my third eye ignited with a vision I have sworn never to reveal.

Amazed, I looked at my grandmother. Her eyes studied mine to see if I had been initiated as she had been so many years ago.

My eyes gave her the answer she sought, as she said, "Well done, child, well done. I think it is time I let you read the scroll."

She handed me the ancient parchment. I held it with great reverence. This paper must have been worth a fortune, I thought, as I held the document of antiquity. My reading of the Greek language was rusty, especially ancient Greek, but my spirit took over where my mind doubted. Slowly I began to decipher the clues the scroll provided about the vision I just had.

The Circle of Olympians

I was not able to fully comprehend this vision. I felt transformed, as if I was in another dimension, yet still in my grandmother's house at the same time. I sipped some coffee hoping the taste and strong caffeine would ground me.

Chapter Four

Destiny

Struggling with the ancient scroll, trying to ground myself to make sense of my vision, my grandmother put her hand on my arm and poured me more coffee. She studied me for an eternal moment, gauging whether or not to reveal more.

I knew that part of the scroll was about me, yet it frightened me. I couldn't deliver the destiny of the sacred text, yet looking in my grandmother's eyes, all was well and I was comforted.

"Calliope, you must trust me and what I am about to tell you," began my grandmother. "You have no choice but to believe in yourself and your destiny. Man becomes insane when he denies his destiny. This is also true for a woman. Once you walk upon a path that is not your own, you are bound to get lost and may never find your way home. Listen to me for I am an old woman and have seen a lot. You know how much I love you, how much I want to protect you, and teach you the ancient ways.

"You are about to see many new things this summer. You must trust me for I would never lead you into harm's way. But there will be others who will try to stop you from fulfilling your mission. I am here to teach you how to protect yourself. Those who mean you harm may not present themselves as dangerous. They

The Circle of Olympians

could come to you as friends, eager for your trust and love. Those are the most dangerous threats to your destiny, but I will teach you in time how to discover and eliminate them from your life. It all depends on your trusting me, and your willingness to follow your destiny to save humanity from its own destruction. From your destiny, there is no escape."

"Grandmother, does it have to be me? How can I help save humanity from destruction?" I pleaded with her.

"Yes, my dear. It is so because that is how it was written thousands of years ago. You know this because you had the same vision I had, the same vision your great grandmother had, and your mother. You are the one who has been chosen by God to be the bridge between humanity and the Divine. You are to be a teacher to show humanity that the only way it will ever survive is through absolute peace and love for one another."

"How can I teach anybody, much less humanity, how to solve the problems of the world? Grandmother, what if I don't want to do it?" I begged.

"You will do it through your writing and after much training and many tests. Do not be afraid. The way you feel is natural. When I first learned of my gifts as a child, I did not want them either. I was so different from my friends and my cousins. I did not want to be special. I did not want to see things or know things, but it was a destiny I could not escape. You will come to terms with your destiny and I will help you."

Euterpe drew the scroll towards her so that she could read a special part to Calliope.

"See here, my dear granddaughter? Look, my angel, this is the part that describes you perfectly. It tells exactly what you are to do and how you will do it. But the author of this scroll was supremely intelligent and wrote it so that only I and members of my family could decipher it. It is not all doom and gloom. It also predicts a beautiful marriage to a man made of dreams. Do you not want that part of your destiny?"

"Grandmother, of course I do, but I feel so unsure of myself. How can I fulfill such a powerful mission? How can I pull off such a monumental feat?"

"Read a little further," Euterpe said as she referred to another part of the scroll. "Here is where it tells of the help you will receive. You will not be alone, but will have help from me, other family members, and from the ancient Olympians who consisted of twelve gods."

"Twelve gods!" I told my grandmother.

"Not all the gods will train you. Only Zeus, Eos, Poseidon, Amphitrite, Apollo, Artemis, Hermes, and Herakles."

My stomach fell to the floor when my grandmother said this. Now I was convinced she was out of her mind and leading me in the same direction. I couldn't disobey her or humiliate her, but how far could I go along with this? Did she honestly think I would believe that the ancient Olympians, the gods and goddesses themselves, would teach me secrets of the universe to help save humanity from complete destruction? Being the master she was, my grandmother looked at me with fire in her eyes, and instantly, I knew she was telling me the truth.

"Forgive me, grandmother. This is all too much for me. We're talking about other dimensions, ancient beings, saving the world, teaching humanity. If that is my destiny, I will accept it, but I need some time."

"We have no time!" she proclaimed.

Chapter Five

Quest

My grandmother wanted to take a walk with me, and sensing I would want to remember what my grandmother was about to tell me, I grabbed my journal and favored pen and threw them into my backpack. My grandmother took her wooden and energetically-charged walking stick, wrapped her head in a black scarf, and told Uncle George we would be back in a while. He understood what we were about to do, and wrapped some cookies and bottled some water for our long trek.

Hiding the amulet and the scroll, my grandmother and I set out on our journey. We walked for about an hour, talking briefly to friends and neighbors to hide the true intent of our steps. We walked behind the local food market into thin woods, and kept walking for what seemed like another hour.

Suddenly, a secret pathway opened up, barely visible to our eyes, but visible to the soul. I had to follow my grandmother's footsteps exactly to know where the path lay. I felt the path more clearly when I closed my eyes. When I looked back for a moment, the path had disappeared behind us. Unexpectedly, we came to a clearing and a wall of rocks. My grandmother closed her eyes and inhaled deeply, settling herself and transporting herself to another dimension. Instinctively

I did as she, but kept peeking to see what was happening. Barely visible, an opening in the rock formed.

"Quickly, child. We must run," my grandmother whispered.

We ran through the opening of the cave as it sealed closed behind us. I was surprised by my grandmother's strength and speed, as she was seemingly aided by her magical walking stick, which cleared the path for her as her feet hit the ground.

Once inside it was pitch dark, but I was not afraid. My grandmother opened her palm, breathed powerfully upon it and ignited a flame to light our way. I nearly collapsed from shock. We still had to walk a bit longer down a winding path visible only from within, deeper into the soul of the hidden mountain. Eventually we saw an ember of a slow burning fire, and I was excited and intrigued by what I was about to discover. More twists and turns and secret passageways led us to the source of this flame.

"You must be very quiet, child, and speak only when I tell you to," my grandmother explained to me. I nodded silently and breathed to center myself.

At the threshold of this sacred place, my grandmother took another settling breath, as if she was keeping the doorway to this other dimension open with her spirit. I followed her and as we walked forward, we crossed the threshold into another world. I couldn't believe my eyes, but sitting on a throne made of rock, was a stunning, ancient woman. She was dressed in black with a shawl on her head. But I could see that she wore her gray hair long. Her face was lined but her eyes of blue were clear and shining with the strength of youth.

Part of my vision flew across my mind, hinting at what may be revealed before me. I felt something deep within my soul stir, yet I didn't know what it all meant. I looked at my grandmother for guidance but she was still deep in meditation, holding the space open for both of us.

As quietly as I could, I felt for my notebook in my backpack. I wanted to record what I was feeling before the spirit and emotion left me. I scribbled a few notes about the cave without revealing its location. I wanted to remember the dampness and the water droplets hanging from the ceiling. I noted the faint smell of ancient incense, a legend I had heard of long ago, and wondered if this was the incense rumored to put people into a prophetic trance. If it was, I didn't want to forget what I might see or experience.

I recorded what I was experiencing without missing anything. I knew that what I was witnessing was important, especially in light of the scroll. Before long, my grandmother came out of her meditation and looked at me intensely, trying to determine if I was ready for what was about to happen.

Chapter Six

Gaea

I couldn't speak, as my speech was taken from me, but in its place was great vision. My grandmother led the way, seeming to float towards a beautiful goddess, who was commanding her domain from atop her mineral throne, deep within the cave. I carefully walked in my grandmother's steps, as I silently watched these two ancient and wise women greet each other.

The flame from my grandmother's hand lit the way, and the three of us formed a circle around a small fire, burning at the foot of the goddess, Gaea. With the flicker of my grandmother's gentle flame lighting our way, I noticed something extraordinary. Gaea looked just like my grandmother! They were identical to one another . . . Gaea was my grandmother's twin!

My mind raced. What could this possibly mean, I wondered to myself. If my Grandmother Euterpe was Gaea's twin, then somehow, I shared the lineage of Gaea, the earth goddess. I felt faint, and as I was about to pass out, my grandmother caught me in her arms. She told me to breathe deeply, trust her, and focus on the light of the flame that burned from the fire at Gaea's feet. Then I heard soft, angelic music, which seemed to come from within the earth. Euterpe's arms were always strong, and held much more than my body at that moment. I began to have a vision and felt safe enough to surrender to it.

The Circle of Olympians

Gaea was the earth goddess worshiped by ancient Greeks as the mother of creation. According to ancient mythology, Gaea gave birth to heaven and the Titans, and was eventually known as the earth mother and goddess.

Legend also held that she was a prophetess, and here she was standing before me, looking exactly like my grandmother. Could she guide my life from the chaos it had become to the serenity of a goddess?

Was the scroll my grandmother held in her hands somehow written by her? She unraveled the scroll before me, beyond what I could see or what I could understand, yet it was up to me to translate part of it for the world. I was able to decipher part of the scroll and some of the drawings, which indicated some world events that had already taken place, but I couldn't figure out what the future held.

I felt faint, as if I was about to lose consciousness. Knowing me so well, and sensing I was at the porthole between this world and another, my grandmother was instantly by my side, and steadied my stance and my being. She held my hands and led me closer to Gaea. Around the fire we sat, staring into its golden red flames and into each other's souls.

Pleading for a rest, deep within the cave, I asked Gaea and my grandmother if I could stay with them for a while and learn from them more of their secrets. Graciously, they agreed.

"Very well, Calliope," said Gaea, "we will talk for a while, and reveal more secrets."

Then Gaea led my grandmother and I in meditation. She sang a beautiful, enchanting song, which hypnotized me into another state. Smoke drifted from the fire towards Heaven and carried our prayers in the form of our thoughts. I had to be very careful what I allowed myself to think. I kept my thoughts pure and focused on how happy and content I was to be with my grandmother and Gaea, my guardian angels.

Gaea stood up and disappeared for a moment. My grandmother and I looked at each other and she assured me with a smile. When Gaea returned, she held in her hand three powerful crystals, glistening in the firelight. My eyes were transfixed on the crystals. I felt an energetic shift in the cave and within myself.

Chapter Seven

Reunion

We were silent for a while, but then my grandmother guided me to reveal the ruby amulet I had been holding in my hand. Cautiously, I revealed the amulet and returned Gaea's gentle smile.

Gaea looked at my grandmother and said, "Welcome, sister." My grandmother embraced her twin and they shared a private moment of the love and symbiosis only twins know. "It has been a long time, but my heart is always filled with your spirit."

Then Gaea looked at me. "She is very beautiful, Euterpe. I have watched her grow over the years and knew the time was right for her to claim her destiny," Gaea said to my grandmother.

I wanted to reach for my writing journal, but knew it wasn't the right time. I hoped I would remember every moment and word that unraveled before me.

"Calliope," my grandmother said, "this is your great Aunt Gaea. You met her once when you were a little girl, but perhaps you do not remember."

Gaea greeted me with the warmth of a long lost relative, and the immediate connection one has with one's own.

"Calliope," said Gaea, "come sit with me dear, so that I may welcome you properly. You are my grand niece. I have watched you grow into a beautiful and powerful woman. It is time for you to take your place and claim your power. I am here to help you understand your purpose in this life and to claim your destiny. Now, would you show me the amulet your grandmother has given you?"

I looked at my grandmother for guidance. She gave her permission with a gentle nod of her head and her steel gaze. I moved closer to Gaea and held out the amulet. It glowed brighter and brighter as it neared the stunning goddess.

The three of us sat in silent unison around the fire, which seemed eternal in the sacred cave. The luminous amulet seemed to know it was time to reveal its secrets. My grandmother and Gaea closed their eyes and inhaled deeply. They continued breathing and invited me to join them, creating a rhythm of joined spirits.

I closed my eyes and concentrated on my breath. The amulet was still in my hand, and heated up to a fiery, scorching temperature. I felt guided by my grandmother and Gaea in our joined silence. Inhaling, I focused on my breath as it traveled deep into my body, swirling around my center, and exhaling warmly through my nostrils. I was unaware that the palm of my hand was being imprinted with the seal of the ruby amulet.

We became one, united in meditation and prayer. Then, a beautiful fragrance joined us, drifting in from another world. I inhaled its intoxicating perfume and felt as if I was leaving my body. A vision began to emerge, deep within my third eye. I knew my grandmother and Gaea were guiding me through this mystical journey and initiation.

In our joint meditation, we traveled through the stars and beyond the planets and galaxies known to humankind. Within seconds, we traveled light years beyond any horizon my eyes or spirit could comprehend. Suddenly, a secret opening appeared in the sky that only my grandmother and Gaea knew. I held my breath and hoped I would be allowed to pass through the threshold. There was a blinding white light, which beckoned us near and invited us to merge with it. As we soared closer, I felt my body, spirit, and mind disappear into this great ocean of love and light. We had passed through many layers of Heaven and were on hallowed ground. I prayed I would remember everything to write in my journal.

Then, the three of us were before God, the Great Spirit and Creator of all things. His benevolence overwhelmed me. No words could express the complete awe I felt being at His feet. My grandmother and Gaea knelt before Him as did I. His power was unquestionable, yet He greeted us as beloved children in His plan.

Holding the amulet steady in the palm of my hand, I knelt before Him, following the women. Sitting upon His throne, He took hold of His ancient scroll, which looked identical to my grandmother's, yet much larger. He loosened the golden ribbon, which held its secrets in place, and carefully unraveled the words He had written upon the parchment so long ago. He looked directly at me and began to read.

Chapter Eight

The Ancient Ones Take Form

We meditated in the Lord's presence and absorbed His words. Then the vision ended and we were back in Gaea's cave. For a moment we were silent, absorbing the word we had all been given.

Gaea told me again that she had watched me all my life. My grandmother and she spent many hours talking about me, and how one day they would train me for my spiritual destiny. They intended to train me that summer in metaphysical, ancient arts, and made me promise to keep my training secret. She told me we would meet daily, and would sometimes disappear for days, but Uncle George would keep our cover. Gaea and Euterpe could cloud people's perception, so if someone witnessed my training, they would not understand what they saw or remember any of it.

And that is how my training with Gaea and my grandmother, Euterpe, began that summer. Almost every day I awoke with the world and the sun at the crack of dawn to meditate. Hours were spent every morning praying to God and listening to His instructions. My grandmother fed me nourishing foods, those that would not cloud my judgment but would add to my developing psychic and physical abilities.

The Circle of Olympians

Each day my grandmother taught me something different: a method of seership, cooking, conserving my physical energy, working with crystals, and how to use any stick of wood as a weapon and teacher.

One day, in Gaea's cave, she and my grandmother reminded me there would be others who will help teach me and test me . . . the ancient Olympians.

"The ancient Olympians? But they're not real. They were part of Greek mythology!" I exclaimed.

"They will be very much part of your life, Calliope," explained Gaea. "They are ancient warriors and children of the ancient gods. They will teach you many skills and much magic."

As Gaea was telling me this, images began to take form within her cave. At first I thought I was seeing things or going out of my mind, but what I saw was real. The ancient Olympians took form within the rock, like Michelangelo's unfinished sculptures, and then came to life, to greet me and eventually train and test me for my life's work.

As if reaching toward me from another dimension, the Olympians climbed forward from the rock and gathered around me. Within moments, I was surrounded by a circle of Olympians. At first I was terrified. Zeus, who ruled all the Olympian gods with his mighty thunderbolt, and his wife, Hera, materialized. Then I recognized all the Olympians. They looked like the drawings I had seen in books on Greek mythology. They were tall, almost ten feet tall, and looked fierce with their armor and helmets and swords. They were staring at me as their forms became manifest from spirit. Each came with a unique gift, a secret to share with me. In turn, I was to learn each gift well and keep it secret. I knew they were to help me save the world from annihilation.

I couldn't see how someone as small and insignificant as I could help save the world, let alone have the honor of meeting and training with the Olympians. My grandmother told me I had to learn to accept things as they were, not as I wanted them to be, so I centered myself and prepared for my formal introduction to the Olympians.

Gaea and Euterpe guided me to put down my notebook and trust them. I was wearing the amulet and felt it light up and empower me.

"Calliope, each one of us will teach you an essential skill," said Gaea. "One will cloak you, another will nourish you, and yet another will teach you to read the minds and thoughts of others, especially those who mean you harm.

"Your training began a long time ago, Calliope, before your birth. All of us have fought the battle you are about to fight, the battle that began long ago. It is the fight for destiny that was written long ago. We must fulfill fate. Since it was written, it must be so," continued Gaea.

Gaea instructed me to wear the amulet at all times, but to keep it hidden. She gave me a gold chain, and helped me put the necklace on with the amulet securely attached. At first it felt warm against my skin. I knew I must never lose it. Gaea read the scroll to me so that I understood every word of instruction within it. My grandmother heard this reading before but listened intently out of respect for her twin. Gaea, with my grandmother, trained me over the course of the summer.

Then, blinding light filled Gaea's cave and I could see nothing else. Hermes, the ancient messenger, suddenly appeared and gave me a cape of protection to wear at all times. Then all at once, I was on earth (yet with them too) in an enchanted forest. I was alone, or so I thought. From my viewpoint, the sky was hidden by the blanket of dew-laden trees. I couldn't see the sun, yet there was Light.

The Circle of Olympians

Even though I felt safe, I drew my sword that Hermes had given me and fastened the collar button of my protective cape. Hermes told me that no harm could come to me beneath this cape. I walked making no sound and breathed with my spirit in silence. All that I knew was with me. Wisdom. I covered my head with my hood and closed my eyes for a moment in prayer. I prayed for protection and vision, and before I opened my eyes, I felt a presence. I sensed huge feet and a being of great weight upon them. Still, I felt safe.

Chapter Nine

ତ୨

Herakles

When I opened my eyes, I saw a broad shouldered and muscular man with dark brown curly hair and bold facial features. By his physique, I could tell he had enormous strength. We looked at each other, standing in the enchanted forest.

"Your first lesson begins," said Herakles.

In the enchanted forest, Herakles held his hands high above his head and instructed me to follow. I put my sword back into its sheath and faced him. He did the same. The sky opened up over our heads. Light poured into us. Into my hands floated a white feather. The feather held great power, and as I clasped my hands around it, my hands began to glow. Herakles smiled and nodded towards my joined hands. I opened them to look at the feather. The feather had become a large ruby.

"You are to learn about power, but your lessons will be in silence. What you see, do not repeat . . . what you feel, hold deep within your being. What you experience, no other will," said Herakles.

I cupped my hands again and closed my eyes for a moment. When I opened my eyes and my hands, the ruby had again become the feather.

"Here, Calliope, take this. Many things will be given to you. Keep everything sacred in this pouch,

The Circle of Olympians

because all that will come to you will be from Him," Herakles said as he gave me a leather medicine bag to put my sacred gifts into.

When I put the blessed pouch on, I felt its powerful aura protect me. I opened the bag and carefully placed the feather inside and gently closed it. Herakles turned as if to lead the way, and a path opened before us, partially hidden by mist.

Through the mist appeared what I thought was a bird, yet he was the same size as I was. His head shone with deep teal colored feathers, gleaned back smoothly. He seemed to be from another dimension . . . part man, part bird. He invited me to shape shift and join him in form.

He said, "Come join me and see everything I see."

Then the birdman disappeared, though only from my eyes as his spirit was still with me. I didn't know what to do. I wanted to see everything I could, and to see everything from the sight of a bird's eyes would be magnificent. I clutched my medicine bag around my neck to feel the spirit of the feather within. What should I do?

As I held my medicine bag, my feet lifted slightly from the ground. I felt the same, yet knew in a way that I was different. I hadn't yet made up my mind and hadn't committed an intention. Could I be sure I could return to my own form? Was the chance to see everything worth possibly losing myself, or my soul? Still, I held the small pouch tightly within my hand.

The feather spoke to my heart, "You can join me in spirit without losing your soul. Trust me and I will lead you home. You do not need to see everything to know that it is there, yet I will show you all you need to see and all that your heart desires."

With those words, my intention was set. I prayed for the Lord's protection, breathed in deeply, and when I exhaled, I had wings.

Sonya Haramis, M. Ed.

The birdman told me many secrets about flying. As I could be in danger when I completed my tests and training . . . moving closer towards my destiny . . . the birdman taught me how to fly and cloak myself from the enemy. I stayed deep within the enchanted forest for a long time, hidden by the sacred mist, training in the art of sacred concealment and flight.

I had to fly by myself for days, sometimes not having a place to land and rest. I had to learn to recognize true birds and false birds, as the false ones could one day try to attack me out of the sky. When I passed the birdman's many tests, I shape shifted back to my original form, and was back in Gaea's cave, absorbing the lesson of flight I had learned with the birdman.

Chapter Ten

ଚ୍ଚ

Zeus

From deep within Gaea's cave, the next one came forward . . . another man of great stature; muscular but with a strength from deep within. His veins pulsated with something other than mere mortal blood.

Before me stood another ancient Olympian. In ancient times, women weren't even allowed to watch the ancient Olympic games, let alone compete in them. How was it that I was about to be trained by them? Piercing into my being with his eyes, I felt faint. Zeus gripped my hand in his so powerfully that my blood felt as if it stopped flowing. His power frightened me, but I had to surrender to the training.

From the ethers within the cave, a flower floated into my free hand. I inhaled deeply and was transported to an ancient forest with Zeus. There I was to learn about my power, both internal and external, through the skill of stone throwing. It would require all the strength I had, as well as control of my center and of my spiral, to throw ancient stones farther than anyone else. I had to prove myself worthy of the task set before me before I could fulfill my destiny.

This ancient training ground held many secrets and benchmarks. I had to learn and surpass all of them. At that moment I wished to give up, but I inhaled the enchanted fragrance of the magical flower, and felt my nerves calm.

Zeus said to me, "You have been chosen from thousands of others to fulfill this task and save humanity from total annihilation. It may seem strange to you that we are here, training in such a seemingly unimportant skill, yet you will need every power and skill I can teach you for your enemies will be fierce and will try to stop and destroy you. You must not let that happen.

"Remember," Zeus warned, " beyond a certain point, we will not be able to help you, so you must train to become the fiercest warrior you can. While we will train in stone throwing as a sport, one day a stone may save your life. It will help train your center, your most powerful muscle. Train it properly and no one will be able to defeat you. Hold this," he said as he handed me a stone. It fit into my hand, yet made my knees buckle and drove me into the ground.

"Stand tall, Calliope. It is essential that you stand tall this moment. Everything depends upon whether or not you can stand tall this minute!"

His command ripped through me. I felt like sobbing because I was overwhelmed by the burden that had been placed on me. Remembering my training in Aikido and other martial arts, and what my grandmother and Gaea had taught me, I breathed into my center, focused my energy, and became one with the stone.

The stone conveyed its essence to me. In a rush, I experienced all that the stone had been through in its evolution to my hand. I felt the rain that once fell upon it, the snow that had once frozen it, the sun that had baked and faded it, and at last, I felt the Source, which created it. I couldn't figure out why the stone was so heavy. What secrets did this ancient relic hold, secrets it may or may not reveal to me? Deep down, I knew that the ancient Olympians were directed by God. I had to obey them.

The Circle of Olympians

"I want you to climb Mount Olympus carrying this stone. If you drop it, all is lost, for I will know you cannot fulfill the destiny entrusted into your hands," Zeus commanded.

Before I could control myself, I burst out laughing and crying at the same time.

"Zeus, I am an empath," I said. "I feel the essence of this stone and have seen its evolution to its present form. I feel its energy and vibration, yet cannot figure out why this small stone is driving me into the ground. It must weigh at least one hundred pounds. While I am not an Olympian or goddess, I have been training hard and I take my destiny and life's calling very seriously. But how am I to climb Mount Olympus when I can barely stand here holding this stone?"

"I will teach you, but before I speak a solemn word of any ancient mystery or secret, you must swear a sacred oath. Once you swear this oath, the path is set before you and you cannot turn back. You must pass every test and task placed before you. If you fail, and especially if you fail after swearing this sacred oath, you not only endanger humankind, but the eternal souls of the immortal Olympians."

I felt faint. The pressure put on me was overwhelming. I had journeyed too far down this road to turn back, yet I was stunned into emotional and mental paralysis. The only thing I could think of was to grasp my amulet with my free hand and call out to my grandmother, my arch protector, and to Gaea, my teacher whose blood ran though my veins.

"Grandmother, help me! I'm overwhelmed, about to break, and I haven't even completed my training. I worked so hard with you. You worked so hard with me and entrusted me with so much. How can I do this? Help me, grandmother, help me Gaea. God, please help me!" I pleaded.

A soft cloud of smoke spiraled towards me carrying my grandmother's perfume. At once, I knew she was with me.

"Calliope, listen to the Voice. It will never mislead you. Even now, during your testing, you must be prepared for deceivers. Trust yourself, and know who speaks the truth. You can do this. I did not raise you and train you to fail. If you fail, you take me with you as well. You must succeed. You must take the oath. You must do what Zeus asks of you," my grandmother instructed.

"Grandmother, how will I do this?"

"Inhale deeply, become one with the stone, take its weight into your own and command a step forward."

I did exactly as she said and took the oath, knowing what she spoke was the truth. As I inhaled, I felt the weight and presence of the stone deep within my center. I felt solid, grounded, and at one with the earth. Though my legs felt immobile, I directed my ki energy down through my center towards my right foot. With every ounce of strength I could gather, with the help of my grandmother and my guardian angels, somehow my right foot moved forward and I began the journey.

Zeus looked at me and smiled. He knew I had received help. I don't think he liked this because he wanted me to be ready to fight and journey on my own. I knew I had to prove myself.

Abruptly, a surge of ki energy ran through my body and I was suddenly walking. Within moments I was running and soon felt as if I was flying. Before me a mist formed. I ran and ran, speed becoming my friend. The mist became dense and I was suddenly in a fog. I couldn't see beyond my own hand, but knew I had to continue running forward and upward.

"Trust yourself, Calliope," my grandmother beckoned me, "and you will find your way."

The Circle of Olympians

I closed my eyes, feeling the stone in my hand and in my center, and drove myself forward. As I ran, I felt ice-cold breezes pass by my head. If I focused on the coldness or my fear, I would be frightened and would fail. This was not an option. Instead I focused on the stone, my breath, my center, my grandmother, and the guardian angels I knew were protecting me.

My legs were burning. My muscles were fatigued beyond exhaustion or beyond the point I had trained. I imagined white light illuminating my veins, feeding my muscles with soothing, healing energy. I remembered my Reiki training, the ancient healing art, and called in the energy I needed.

I then felt a sudden force try to block me from going one more step forward. It was as if I had hit a wall of energy I couldn't penetrate. This was a challenge to my mind. I visualized the blockage cleared away, yet nothing happened. I altered my emotional vibration that matched a clear path, yet still nothing happened.

I inhaled and exhaled with a powerful kiai to unify all of my being and strength, yet still nothing happened. I quieted myself for a moment, inhaled deeply three times and cleared my breath. Gradually, I received the answer in a vision. Once more I inhaled as deeply as I could, and when I exhaled I hurled the stone with all my might, releasing it after I had spiraled in a circle like the ancient discus throwers. I heard an audible pop, felt an opening clear, and then heard the stone land. As I had attached its energy to my center, the stone pulled me through the cloud and instantly I was atop Mount Olympus.

The panoramic view was astonishing. In one moment I knew that all the legends, all the myths, all the stories and secrets of the gods were true. Somehow I had been entrusted to experience this. Somehow, I was allowed behind the veil.

"Well done, Calliope. Well done!" cried Zeus.

Chapter Eleven

༄

Amphitrite

I was back in Gaea's cave when another Olympian took form, this time a woman. As she came forward and as she drew closer, I felt the ocean water gather at my feet. The water line kept inching up my body, the water becoming deeper by the moment.

"You must trust me," said Amphitrite, Poseidon's wife. "Take my hand, Calliope, take one final breath, and let go."

There was no other choice but to surrender to her. I inhaled deeply, took her hand and let go. "Will I survive this?" I asked with my final breath.

I found myself floating in the ocean and Amphitrite spoke to me. I stared up at the monolithic mountain eager to hear the words meant for me. The salt held me in the water as I closed my eyes to hear the Silence. Beneath the water's surface lay the answer to all questions.

"You are to learn about the water and currents," Amphitrite said.

I was lifted and swayed by the hands of the water. Gently, all my worries were worked away by the flow of the water. Its ki moved through me and around me filling me with its spirit, its energy. I felt the blue of its power enter my body and I saw blue light through my third eye. A voice spoke to me.

The Circle of Olympians

"You do not always know where I will lead you, or where the current of life will take you, but you must release yourself to it if you are to journey at all. Surrender the end to me, and you will enjoy ceaseless beginnings. All will unfold anew every day, if you allow it to. As you cannot clutch my water in your hands, you cannot clutch time or events. You cannot direct the tide, but only follow it. If you trust that it will lead you to your heart's desire, then it will. If you try to clutch its flow, you will stop the course of your life. Take one last breath and go beneath the water's surface again."

Together, we rushed through the vast Aegean Sea, deeper and deeper until the bottom of the ocean was within reach. Why wasn't I dead yet, I wondered. I had embarked on a journey whose end was not in my control, but had to surrender to it to survive it.

The currents of the deep ocean swayed back and forth, up and down, caressing my body and welcoming me into its kingdom. Pulsating rhythms hypnotized me beyond my fears and beyond my questions.

Schools of fish began to gather near us. Millions of fish swam around us, creating a vortex from all corners of the earth, answering a silent cry. Creatures I had never seen before were swimming over my head. Species of all shapes and sizes, colors and forms swam around us creating a whirlpool. As we were drawn deeper into the whirlpool, I felt as if I was becoming like a fish. I felt as if I could breathe through openings on the side of my body. My vision began to clear and I felt sleek and aerodynamic. Was I shape shifting?

Amphitrite was still holding my hand and swimming in the circle of millions of fish with me. She smiled at me assuredly and squeezed my hand. So many emotions ran through me. While I was swimming with millions of fish at the bottom of the Aegean, perhaps shape shifting into a fish, I felt at the same time that I was part of an ancient Greek dance, the steps we still dance.

Was all life a dance? Did all of us join with one another, either in song or in stroke, to share the same circle and spiral that leads us to the center of all things, all that is? Instinctively I felt that this was part of the lesson I was to learn with Amphitrite.

My head began to swirl. I felt nauseous. Amphitrite held my hand and sensed my discomfort. I couldn't pass out. I couldn't fail at one thing for if I did, all was lost. Amphitrite stopped me for a moment, floating in the depths of the currents that swam around us. She looked deeply into my eyes, pressed my third eye with her thumb and breathed into it. I felt my ribs open and move, as Amphitrite had created gills on my side.

"Breathe. Allow the water to be your oxygen . . . allow it to be your life. Surrender to it and you will live," she said to me.

I inhaled the water deep into my being. It filled me with serenity and my mind cleared. My dizziness left me, and my vision cleared.

Amphitrite held my hand again and we joined the flow of fish once more. Suddenly, the ocean floor opened up and a great temple emerged. It looked like a glistening crystal cathedral with shiny, prismatic hues of aqua blue and silver. There were no windows or closed doors, and the fish freely swam within and around the great temple beneath the water. A Presence made himself known before he made himself visible. He was benevolent yet powerful.

Amphitrite held my hand and we swam into the depths and center of the temple. All the fish, connected energetically to the great temple, expanded their circle to make room for the divine home. I looked all around and was struck by the glistening

The Circle of Olympians

gemstones that radiated from its walls: aquamarine, sapphire, lapis, quartz, blue diamonds, and more. I never before had seen anything so beautiful in my life. I hoped I would remember all of this to write in my journal and share with the world.

I then realized Amphitrite's breastplate was covered with these same stones and that she was wearing a bracelet to match.

"Close your eyes, Calliope, and don't open them until I tell you to," she guided me.

I closed my eyes nervously. "Trust . . . surrender" I repeated to myself, echoing my grandmother's advice.

The water began to pulsate feverishly and bubbles stormed skyward all around us. It felt as if the bottom of the ocean and the earth itself was about to explode. Keep your eyes closed, I told myself. I had to focus or I would have been swallowed by the ocean. Tranquility emerged in an instant as Amphitrite squeezed my hand.

"Open your eyes, Calliope. It is safe now to look clearly before you," she instructed.

I blacked out for a moment, but when I was conscious again I was in a crystal palace of aquamarine and blue sapphire. As I opened my eyes, there he was before me on his throne, trident in hand. Poseidon! I couldn't believe it. Once again, all the legends and myths were true. He was sitting upon his jewel-encrusted throne, trident firmly in his hand, directing the universe of the sea.

"Welcome Amphitrite and Calliope. It is a great honor that you decided to join us, Calliope. You have great courage to have come this far and great challenges await you, but we will teach you how to win each battle you are forced to fight. You will be victorious. Great and ancient secrets of the sea will be revealed to you, but you must swear an oath of honor never to reveal or betray a secret. You are the only mortal who will be given this vast knowledge. Guard it well, guard it with your life," warned Poseidon.

He continued, "My legion will teach you well. Pay attention, for the lessons will be over in what will seem like an instant. Once you seal your oath and vow, there is no going back."

"Greetings, Poseidon, I have gone to great trouble to bring Calliope before you. She has been well trained and is well prepared. She will not fail," said Amphitrite.

Poseidon spoke again, "I watch over all beings who dwell within the sea and know what goes on at all times. With one swift cut of my trident, I can change the course of humankind and destiny. It is I who brought you here. You can always call upon me for guidance and sustenance when you are lost and do not know your way. With one cut of my spear, I can change your life. All you need to do is ask, but once you have asked, release your wish to me so that I can answer it. You cannot answer your own prayer. Feel the smoothness of the waters and release yourself. Flow with the current of life and become one with the Universe and the ki of the ocean."

He gave me a perfect, radiant shell to hold in my medicine pouch. With it, I would always have a connection to Poseidon whenever I needed it. There was an energy building in my medicine bag. I could feel it. There was also an energy building within me. Every moment, every meeting with an ancient Olympian was changing me, empowering me, filling me with knowledge and Spirit.

"Calliope, are you ready?" asked Poseidon. "Time for you to go, but we will meet again."

I thanked Poseidon for his gift and wisdom and promised to return, although it was up to him when I could do so.

The Circle of Olympians

Everything inside me wanted to run, certain I couldn't fulfill what was being asked of me. Just at that moment a school of dolphins swam around me, soothing my nerves with their presence. One, apparently the leader, brushed alongside me as if to introduce himself to me. Gently, he led me forward and the school surrounded us, guarding me from any danger.

Amphitrite let go of my hand and I shape shifted into a dolphin to conceal my identity. (Apparently I wasn't the only one who was now aware of my destiny.) I had heard of this shaman art but never thought I could do it or experience it. Interestingly, I felt the same as I always had. From the time I was a little girl, I loved the water and felt free immersed in it. The dolphins swam on, and I followed unsure of where we were going or what I would learn.

We began to swim faster, for even though I shape shifted into a dolphin, someone was aware of my presence and wanted to stop me from getting to wherever it was we were going. Two very large warrior dolphins immediately flanked my sides. The school around us started swimming in patterns to divert and confuse the approaching enemy. Their movements woke up the sand and created a wall impenetrable by eyes. Yet, the current still seemed disturbed by a fierce undercurrent. I was terrified. Amphitrite was still close to me and whispered to me that I shouldn't be afraid. How could I control my fear when I was terrified?

I suddenly heard my grandmother's voice. "Calliope, you must not be afraid for your fear will draw that which you fear to you. Remember your training! Breathe, trust, surrender, and pray," she commanded.

Somehow my grandmother was watching me so I wasn't in complete danger, but I was still terrified. I did as she said. I breathed deep into my being. I trusted my protectors, my new friends the dolphins, my own ability, and above all . . . God. I prayed to Him and surrendered to Him, knowing I was powerless without Him.

Out of the depths of the deep ocean, a great white shark suddenly burst into our territory. In one instant, I knew the shark was looking for me. I saw it before it saw me. My dolphin friends swam faster, determined to protect me. In the distance there was a faint, dim light. That light was our goal.

I felt myself hyperventilating, but if I allowed myself to panic I would give myself away. I prayed to God to help me, asking Him to help me surrender to Him and to trust myself. I had to fully own my power, even if I was sure I had none. I inhaled deeply, felt the power of my new, temporary form, and trusted the dolphins around me to lead me to the light ahead of us. The shark tried to attack one of the dolphins, but its wisdom and foresight protected it. The shark was unable to attack any of us for we all bonded together and became impenetrable. I centered myself. I knew if I didn't look the shark in the eye, it couldn't take my power. Why was I tempted to look at it, even though I knew it would mean my doom?

"Calliope, don't be a fool!" my grandmother's voice yelled out to me.

Jolted out of my potential stupidity, I held onto Amphitrite's hand, kept my focus on the inner circle of the school I was swimming with, and the light ahead. All else began to disappear. My fear began to leave me as I was overcome with joy and tranquility. Then, as if empowered by the release of my fear, all of us swam in an instant to the light. A secret doorway opened, just enough to let us through, and sealed up as soon as all of us were through it, closing out the shark.

* * *

The Circle of Olympians

Shocked, I stopped swimming to catch my breath, and contemplated what we had just gone through and what it meant. Someone, somewhere, was aware of my destiny and wanted to stop me. And they were a gifted sorcerer, to be able to shape shift to cause fear and terror. I thanked my dolphin friends and Amphitrite for protecting me, but worried what I would have done had they not been there to answer my prayer to God.

It dawned on me that we were in another part of the deep sea. Ancient, secret, yet somehow familiar to me. I allowed the gentle currents to carry me where it wanted me to go, as I had to surrender to the water and to the light that saved my life. I closed my eyes to hear my soul. Amphitrite swam to my side, took my hand and led me to a hidden altar made of shells and gemstones.

"Calliope, I felt your fear, but you handled it well. You must remember how to control your fear, because you will need to control it again. I did not want to tell you this before we began our journey, but there is another who is aware of your destiny and who wants to stop you. They want to control the destiny of humankind, and know that if you succeed, they will die. If they can stop you, they will control the fate of humanity, and turn the world into an empire of evil," warned Amphitrite.

Devastated, I cried out for my grandmother. "Grandmother, help me. Don't leave me alone. I cannot handle this by myself. I'm too afraid."

From behind the altar, my grandmother miraculously swam out in front of me.

"My dearest Calliope. My little bird. Don't you know by now that you are not alone, that we are ever present, guiding your every step? Surely you must know that I hear your every cry for help, every prayer, every doubt? I know because I have watched you grow from the first moment you were born. This is your destiny and you cannot escape it. It is true, there is another who wants to stop you . . . to stop us. She is an ancient enemy of our family and of our bloodline, and her vendetta goes way back," said my grandmother.

"Years ago," she continued, "there was a competition among the ancient women of truth and knowledge, a sort of metaphysical contest, the winner of which won the honor to possess the amulet now in your possession. There were many hard tests, and through great courage, effort, prayer, and faith, I won. Our enemy was furious and has wanted to gain possession of the amulet ever since. I have not revealed all the powers of the amulet to you yet, because you have to go through the same tests I went through to prove you are worthy. My dearest granddaughter, I know you are worthy, but you have to prove it to God and to the Olympians, the guardians of all these secrets and powers, so that it can remain in our family, and therefore save the world from this evil power. We must guard you, conceal you, and protect you until you fulfill your mission," comforted my grandmother.

I sobbed in her arms, shape shifting back to my true self, while she cradled me and continued, "We had to see if you could shape shift, and if you could swim as the dolphins. Years ago, the Minoans believed the dolphins had special psychic powers and healing abilities. Today, most people do not believe that, but dolphins are special and evolved beings. They hold many secrets, and many of them will be revealed to you now. We had to see if you could truly surrender to your power, to God . . . if you could control your fear, and focus on the light of God. You have been victorious, Calliope, but you must keep your guard up, for the enemy will return.

The Circle of Olympians

"Now I want to show you something else," continued Euterpe.

The dolphins and Amphitrite gathered around us as Euterpe held out a shell to me. Amphitrite studied the shell and knew what it was to be used for.

"Calliope, you may use this shell to call forth the help of these dolphins any time you need help. Keep it in your medicine pouch, and use it wisely," warned my grandmother.

Amphitrite recognized the shell as one she had used often, and spoke of her gratitude towards the dolphin tribe that had saved her own life many times.

"These dolphins are our eternal friends," instructed Amphitrite. "They will put their own lives in danger to protect us, Calliope, and for this you must serve them well. When your testing is complete and your work is done, you must remember to help and protect them for they need your guardianship. There are others who would like to destroy them, but you must not allow that to happen."

I vowed to protect my new dolphin friends and guardians. To this day I look for them in the deep blue waters of the oceans of the world.

Chapter Twelve

Destined Journey

Back in Gaea's cave, I felt overwhelmed and needed to rest. I took the shell from my grandmother, and held it in my hand. I lay my head on her lap, contemplating what had been shared with me. I understood if I were ever in trouble in the deep oceans, I could use the shell to call my dolphin friends and they would come to my rescue.

I had passed one of my tests, controlling my fear and focusing my attention on the Light rather than on my fear. I was uneasy learning of an ancient enemy hunting me for my amulet and my destiny. I wished there was a way I could abdicate this heavy burden, but knew I could not turn back since I had taken several sacred oaths. I lay my head on my grandmother's lap.

Exhausted, I begged for rest from my tests and training with the Olympians. My mind and spirit couldn't absorb any more and I needed to rest, and forget about the duty that had been placed on my shoulders and in my heart. I begged my grandmother for rest, and she looked to Gaea for direction. With a nod and firm grasp upon her staff, Gaea granted me permission to rest for a while.

"Calliope, there is something you should know about your grandmother. Now may be the right time

The Circle of Olympians

for you to find out. She kept her true identity secret from you all these years to protect you, so do not get angry when you learn of her true powers. There are already mighty forces of evil trying to stop you from completing your life's work. We must not let that happen. We have to remain ahead of them, and cloak your true identity and family lineage as long as possible. Come quickly!" Gaea commanded me.

She hurriedly gathered a medicine pouch, some sacred stones and crystals, some clothes, her walking staff (for walking and protection) and the scroll.

"We are going to a place that only women are allowed to enter. You must remain alert and aware at all times, for until we are within the inner chamber of the Sacred Grove, you will not be safe. Once we are there, you will be able to rest, but until then, Calliope, be prepared," Gaea warned.

The last thing I felt like doing was going on another dangerous trek through the wilderness, while someone was hunting me, trying to stop me from fulfilling my life's work. I couldn't believe I was so important to the fate of humankind. How did I get myself into this and how could I quickly get out of it, I wondered? If I could sneak out of Gaea's cave and get to the harbor of Ithaca, I could get on a boat, get to the airport and take the first plane back to California. I just couldn't handle anything more. I looked at my savvy grandmother who knew exactly what I was thinking.

"My dear Calliope," she said. "You cannot escape who you were born to be. If you fight your destiny, you create a doorway for evil to enter. Even if you do not realize or believe how important you are, we do, and it is our destiny to protect you until you are trained in the arts that will lead to victory. You are fighting not only for yourself, Calliope, but also for the soul of humanity, who have lost their way. The Creator and the gods devised this ingenious plan to save humanity, but only if you succeed. Generations of our family have trained in secret waiting for this time, this exact moment, when only you could save humanity. You have no choice, but I can help you handle your burden with greater ease if you let me.

"Do not dread the journey to the Sacred Grove," my grandmother comforted. "The grove is a sacred place, set aside especially for women who need to restore their soul and strength and energy. The journey will be dangerous only if you allow it to be. Do not focus on the threat of what could be, focus on the peace you will find once you enter the enchanted forest of peace and restoration. I know, Calliope, for I have been there many times. Wear your amulet and you will be invisible. Only your fear will give you away, so hide it well, and focus on the Sacred Grove. When you feel afraid, listen for my voice, take comfort in my spirit, and know you are not alone. Come, gather your things. We must go now."

Exhausted but intrigued, I gathered my things from Gaea's cave. I checked to make sure I was wearing my amulet, gathered some clothes, an extra sweater, a blanket, some water, and stuffed my journal and pen into my backpack. I took a deep breath. I wanted to look at my reflection in a small pond deep within Gaea's cave, yet when I stood before the still silent water, I saw nothing.

I gasped, but my grandmother steadied me by the arm, and whispered in my ear, "Remember my darling, you are invisible. Only your fear can betray you while you are wearing the amulet. Guard it with your life, and remember to focus on the peace and rest that awaits you in the Sacred Grove."

I looked at my grandmother and gently kissed her cheek. What would I ever do without her, I wondered, not ever wanting to find out.

The Circle of Olympians

Gaea led the way. My grandmother walked behind me, protecting me from harm from any direction. Through many secret pathways we walked out of the cave, passing ancient and tiny guardians as we walked. They were all there to guard the sacred earth Gaea ruled over.

I still couldn't believe the mission I had to fulfill, but I had to guard my thoughts and forced myself back to the present moment. I focused on each step, carefully watching where I was putting my feet. At the same time, I had to make sure I didn't lose sight of Gaea, while controlling my fear. It was dark within Gaea's world, so dark I could barely see an inch ahead of me, but I focused on Gaea and her spirit, and was guided by her energy. I almost slipped and fell a number of times, but my grandmother kept me steady. Besides, she knew this path from many journeys she had made upon it.

Suddenly, Gaea looked startled and instructed us to freeze where we were until she said otherwise. She went ahead to investigate a sound she heard that disturbed her deeply.

"Do not be afraid, Calliope," my grandmother whispered.

I was terrified. I knew Gaea was a powerful goddess. If she was frightened by something, then it must be terrifying. I fought to control my escalating fear and my breathing, and to remain still. My grandmother and I breathed together, as she guided me in a visualization of the Sacred Grove. It sounded more beautiful than I could ever have imagined. I couldn't wait to get there and be safe. With my beloved grandmother, I focused on the grove until I felt it with every part of my being. At that moment, Gaea returned.

"They have found us, and they know where we are going. We must return to the cave." warned Gaea. Once within the safety of the cave Gaea spoke. "I knew this would be difficult, but we are not alone and must call on the gods to assist us. I overheard them plotting to capture Calliope, after they follow us to the Sacred Grove. Calliope, they not only want to stop you but they want to destroy any paradise the Creator has made for us. We must not allow this to happen. We have a choice to make: we can divide ourselves and I can become a decoy, or we can retreat and try to go another time, or we can continue now together. Whatever we choose we must call upon the gods to help us now! Calliope, you must decide!" Gaea demanded.

Stunned by her command, I was terrified to make a decision. How could I know what to do? I didn't know how to call upon the gods. I had just started my training, and was exhausted beyond the breaking point. I wasn't ready to put any of it to use, not at that moment, and not with so many lives at stake.

"Calliope, you must decide," my grandmother prodded.

I thought about the dolphins, and what they taught me. I thought about walking up Mount Olympus with the stone I couldn't carry, yet somehow managed to climb to the peak carrying it. I contemplated my destiny and the fate of humanity. I knew I had to go on. From deep within my center and with all my heart, I called upon the Divine and asked for His help through the intervention of the gods.

"Lord, please help us. I need your help. Please! I'm begging you. We need your protection, Lord, if I am to fulfill the destiny you have chosen for me," I pleaded.

Even though I was invisible, cloaked by the amulet, and my grandmother and Gaea were both masters with great power, I was desperate for divine intervention. Miraculously, a white mist began to form before us. A sweet smell accompanied the form taking shape, and the great warrior appeared before us . . . Artemis.

Chapter Thirteen

༄

Artemis

Artemis, daughter of Zeus and twin of Apollo . . . the goddess who caught my eye through her stars across the sky . . . was the next Olympian. She took form as I meditated deep within Gaea's cave.

She beckoned me with her lights and I answered her with my gaze. I was lost in her land, the land that dwelt within the horizon of our dreams.

Her shooting stars pierced the sky. Somehow I felt each one before they took flight. My breath and my heart were taken with each flying light. In the wind, Artemis whispered to me to fly with the next star that flew by me. As I felt the next shooting star about to come, I readied my hands to grab hold of it as it flew by me.

I clutched my medicine pouch, which held the feather of flight, and said a prayer. I was lifted gently into her sky and suspended in her hands. I felt the star coming as the wind blew, blowing my hair and my protective cape nearly off my body. I outstretched my arms and opened my eyes, including my third eye.

All at once, the star flew past me. I caught its tail and hung on with all the strength I had within me. I climbed the length of its tail until I reached the aura and center of the star. I inhaled deeply and when I exhaled, I grabbed the star with my open palms and sealed my being to it. The star and I became one.

We flew for thousands of miles. The sky changed from deep, midnight blue to rose pink, the color of rebirth and reconciliation. All other stars lay at the feet of the goddess, suspended in the air of her breath. It seemed as if they were waiting for something from her, that they had flown to her (perhaps called by her) across the universe, across time and through many dimensions, to be by her side. Perhaps they were there to answer her call or need, whatever that may be. There I waited, sealed to the star, and I, too, felt pulled home.

"You are to learn about Light," Artemis said. "Gently close your right hand to gather a bit of star dust. Swallow a small bit and put the rest in your medicine bag."

I did as she told me and as I closed my right hand, the star felt soft and smooth and melted easily within my grasp. I tasted a bit of the stardust and swallowed a small, sweet amount. With great care I poured the rest of the stardust into my medicine bag and closed it tight.

I looked at my belly and saw a swirling ray of Light moving through my body. It felt warm and good and healing. When it reached my head, my inner eye exploded with Light. I then knew that I lived within the Light, and that it lived within me, and was eager to help me with whatever lesson I needed to learn. I knew that it would always be there to protect me, nurture me, and guide me forever.

"Whenever you wish to call upon the Light, focus on your center. The Light is always there, but you can call upon it for protection. Calliope, you carry the Light with you always. Once you learn to bring it up into your third eye at will, you can ask for anything and it will manifest," said Artemis.

"I will help you, Calliope. It is my duty to guard and protect women, especially the young and vulnerable, as well as to protect animals. No one under my guard will

The Circle of Olympians

be harmed, but we must wait for the right time to journey to the Sacred Grove. I will call my legion of priestess warriors to help us, and consult the phase of the moon to know the perfect time to begin our journey. My animals will help us, and destroy those who mean us harm," Artemis proclaimed.

I couldn't believe Artemis came to help us. I should have had an offering, but was empty handed.

"Artemis, thank you for coming to help us. I am empty handed, but am filled with gratitude for your help," I explained.

"Do not fret, Calliope. There will be time for offerings and celebrations. Now is not the time. Stay here with your grandmother and Gaea, while I meditate and consult the phase of the moon," Artemis instructed.

"Grandmother, Gaea, I'm afraid. What do we do now?" I asked.

"Do not be afraid, Calliope. Nothing will happen to us. We are divinely protected, and all that we must do is follow Artemis' direction. Let us meditate together, calm our nerves, and breathe with the earth," Gaea said.

We put our things down and sat upon the dewy earth, deep within Gaea's cave. We held hands and sat in a circle, facing one another. Gaea began the meditation with one deep breath. My grandmother joined in with her inhalation and exhalation. Then I joined them, and in unison we breathed together as one spirit.

It felt as if we sat in meditation for days, until Artemis returned. When she did she explained that we had to wait until the eclipse of the moon that would help cloak us, and my fear, until we safely reached the Sacred Grove. We waited a few nights, and then Artemis told us it was time to leave for the Sacred Grove.

"Now, we must hurry," she said as she gathered her arrows in her bag, slung over her shoulder as it had been for thousands of years.

"Calliope, before we embark on our journey, I want to teach you how to shoot an arrow. You may need to defend yourself one day when I am not near," Artemis told me.

"Artemis, how will I remain invisible if I carry a bow and arrows? How can I learn to shoot an arrow when we have to go now?" I pleaded.

"Do not worry, for as long as you wear your amulet, the bow and arrows, and anything else you carry, will be invisible too. Only if your amulet is struck from you or when you take it off will you become visible. And I will teach you very quickly how to load and shoot an arrow. Remember, Calliope, you already know how to do it. You are a born huntress!" Artemis encouraged.

"Gaea, Euterpe, go on ahead and wait for us at the mouth of the cave," Artemis commanded. "My priestess warriors are guarding the entrance to this cave. We will be there shortly. I must first teach Calliope how to shoot an arrow, in case she needs to protect herself."

"Guard her well, Artemis, for we love her desperately, and everything rests upon her shoulders and her destiny," my grandmother begged.

"We will do as you say, Artemis. Remember you can call on me through the earth. If you need my help, I am here," promised Gaea.

"Go now, and do not worry. I promise to guard Calliope with my life, but I feel led to teach this skill now," Artemis said.

Artemis took me by the hand as my grandmother and Gaea both kissed me on the cheek and hugged me. Artemis and I watched my grandmother and Gaea walk through secret passageways to an opening I could barely see, but for a hint of light. I clutched my amulet, and breathed deep into my center, hoping I would succeed in the archery lesson before me.

From her bag of arrows slung over her shoulder, Artemis drew a smaller, golden bow, which was the perfect size for me. She presented it to me with a gleam in her eye, and produced a special arrow.

"Take this bow. Hold it. Feel it. Breathe with it. It is yours and you must know it as you know your own hand," Artemis whispered.

I held the weighty bow in my hand. It was strangely familiar to me. It was heavier than I anticipated, yet knew its weight was necessary to carry its swift and fierce arrows. I held the handle of the bow in my left hand, held it up to eye level, and drew the bow to get a feel for the weapon. It felt familiar. Artemis was right, I did know how to shoot an arrow from this bow, and had done so before, but had no conscious memory of it. Holding the bow, I closed my eyes and breathed into it.

"Well done. I can see that you remember, Calliope, but not everything. You have always needed to work on your aim, and that has to do with your intention. Your focus must be clear in order to hit your target. You have struggled with this before, but you cannot miss any target now, as the stakes are too high for all of us," Artemis cautioned.

"Your hand must never leave your bow when you are defending yourself or others. The bow represents your spirit, your intention, and if you are being hunted, you must never allow your spirit to believe it is prey. You will never be prey, even though there are those who would like to defeat you. You must know that you are unstoppable, and that you and your bow are inseparable. I want you to cherish this bow, protect it, own it as yours, and guard it with your life. It will serve you well.

"You must focus, and put your ki energy into the bow from your center, down your arm and into the bow and arrow. Inhale from the earth through your feet and up through your body when you draw the bow. Focus your ki into the arrow as you fill your center with your breath. Know that nothing can disturb your concentration as you draw the arrow and find your target. Only when you are certain you have become one with your target should you release the arrow and your intention. Watch me," Artemis invited.

She held her mighty bow in her hand. She drew a silver arrow, and expertly loaded it into her bow. (I heard about her silver arrows, and was awed to learn they were actually real and before me.) She inhaled deeply, as if consuming all of the air living within Gaea's cave. For a moment, I felt choked and gasped for air. She waved her free hand and above us the earth of the cave opened up revealing the sky. Off in the distance, I could faintly see a tree in a beautiful forest.

Then, Artemis released the glimmering arrow. It seemed to travel thousands of miles. It struck a piece of fruit dangling from the tree so far away. I couldn't believe it! When Artemis shot the arrow, she seemed to release a part of herself with it. She shot the arrow with every part of her being and became one with the bow. She focused her entire spirit on her target, yet was aware of everything else around her. She released the arrow at the perfect time.

"I shot my arrow into the fruit of that tree," Artemis explained. "I meant no harm to this tree and therefore no harm will come to it, but I wanted to show you how to focus your attention while you release your arrow. Pick up your bow, Calliope, and aim for a piece of fruit."

I picked up my bow, felt it in my hand, centered myself, and completely attached my energy to the bow. I breathed into my center and focused my ki energy through my arm, into my hand, and onto the handle of the bow. I used a silver arrow Artemis gave me. I held it at eye level and drew the bow. My hands began to shake, as I unexpectedly felt too weak to draw the bow completely.

"Focus, Calliope, you must focus your attention," Artemis warned.

All my fears and self doubt swiftly surfaced as I felt I couldn't do it. As my doubt grew, the opening in the sky began to close.

"Your fear and self doubt affect millions of others' lives, not just your own, Calliope. You cannot afford to doubt yourself or the help you are receiving. Release your fear, forgive your self doubt, and embrace the power and love that await you," Artemis commanded.

I had to win over my fear and self doubt. I had to draw the bow as a symbol of claiming my power and support from the Divine and the gods. I inhaled and repeated to myself over and over again Artemis' words, as well as the words of my grandmother. "I must do this" I convinced myself. I breathed in, asked for help, and drew the bow an inch farther. Through my pain, I focused my ki energy and kept my eye on the target before me. I chose a ripe piece of fruit and became one with it. At the right moment, I released the bow and my energy with it. The arrow soared through the sky and plunged perfectly into the center of the ripe fruit.

"Well done, Calliope! Well done," exclaimed Artemis, smiling proudly and with great relief. "Now I know you will be safe," she sighed. "We must go now."

At that moment, as Artemis shifted her attention, the opening that revealed the sky overhead closed. She put her bow in her bag and slung it over her shoulder. She gave me a smaller, similar bag, and guided me to do the same. Quickly, I followed her lead and her step as she speedily progressed towards my grandmother and Gaea.

Within moments, we were by their side. I embraced my grandmother. Though I had trained hard thus far, I was still nervous and unsure of my abilities and the task before me. Artemis, Gaea, my grandmother, and I held hands. We said a prayer of thanks and asked for protection for our journey. We left an offering of laurel to the earth and vowed to return to Gaea's cave victoriously.

"Everything will be all right, Calliope, I promise," said my grandmother.

"Remember who you are, Calliope, and all will be well," encouraged Gaea. "Remember also that you are not alone. While your fate and destiny are yours to bear, you have help and will be guided along the way by secrets, whispers, miracles, and magic. Remember this.

I tried to calm my nerves and said a special prayer to the Divine. I asked for courage and comfort, and asked the Divine to walk with us. From deep within the core of the earth, a gentle and warm breeze floated by us. I knew at that moment we would be safe.

"I am ready," I declared.

Chapter Fourteen

Eos

With Gaea leading the way, I, along with my grandmother and Artemis behind me, left the safety of Gaea's cave. As soon as we were outside of the cave, a frosty and damp wind whipped down upon us, yet I was not afraid. I had been prepared well and refused to surrender to my fear. Whose spirit this chill was I couldn't tell, nor was I sure who sent it, but suspected it was our enemy, so I chose not to give it my energy or attention.

Unexpectedly, Eos, the beautiful dawn, and mother of the wind and stars, greeted us with her abundance of love and light.

"My precious Calliope, I have come to light the way for your journey to the Sacred Grove. No harm will come to you, as I have chased away the dark spirit that was here a moment ago. This spirit is an ancient enemy who fears you because it knows you will defeat it once and for all. You are well guarded, well loved, and you will be victorious," Eos said to me as she kissed my cheek.

"Gaea, lead the way. I will light our path with my light and the stars, but take the hidden path," Eos cautioned.

Gaea nodded to Eos, then held up her hands, closed her eyes, and said a silent prayer. As she opened her eyes, just ahead of us a path appeared that wasn't there before.

"We must go quickly for this path will not remain visible to us for long," Gaea said to all of us.

Eos' light illuminated the revealed path. We walked in sacred steps, one behind the other to hide our numbers so that it appeared there was only one of us walking. As soon as we were on the path, I looked behind us and saw that the opening we had walked through had sealed up. Truly, it was hidden and sacred, and had been revealed only to us.

I felt completely safe. I loved these women, and felt guarded and protected by them. I suddenly missed my mother. I wished she was there with me, but was relieved she was safe at home in California. The stress of this journey would have been too much for her to handle, and she would have worried about me too much.

Never before had I been in the presence of such extraordinary women, goddesses, and powerful warriors. I was thrilled to be in their presence and wanted to sear every moment into my memory and soul. What gifts I had been given: the training, the journey, the scroll, the amulet, my grandmother, Uncle George, my mother, Gaea, Artemis, and now Eos. Unbelievable! In that summer I learned that miracles truly did happen.

We continued walking on the hidden path for what seemed like hours. The ground beneath our feet was soft and nurturing, and the animals around us were loving and kind . . . friends and wards of Artemis. The birds sung eloquently and chirped their beautiful songs, serenading us every step of the way. Eos' beautiful dawn lit the journey for us the entire way, shielding me from my internal fear as well as any external fears. The air was moist with special dew. It caressed my skin and conditioned my hair and intoxicated my spirit. What land had I been privileged to come to?

"We are almost there, Calliope," Gaea whispered. "It is just a few steps ahead and then you will be able to fully rest."

Just ahead of us I saw a thick forest. I had read about ancient sacred groves, but never thought I would have the honor to walk within one, or that one would even still exist.

"From this point on we must be very quiet," warned Gaea, "for we must not reveal the doorway to the Sacred Grove to anyone."

With her hand covering her mouth, she turned to us and gestured our need for complete silence. We nodded in response as we silently approached the green heaven. As we neared the grove, the air became sweeter and lighter, and my head filled with a joy it had never known. My spirit was uplifted and I wanted to float in the air. I was so filled with happiness that I understood what it meant to be overflowing with joy. I concentrated on my breath and made sure to breathe silently, determined not to reveal the location of the secret grove.

All the trees looked the same to me, but Gaea was looking for a special one that would open the doorway to the Sacred Grove. She then revealed a crystal from her medicine pouch she was wearing around her neck. It was a magnificent clear crystal, cut in a special way, which was in some way a key. She closed her eyes, connected with the crystal, breathed deeply, and exhaled when she opened her eyes, looking for the opening to the Sacred Grove. Magically, the opening appeared. It was barely visible, but it was clearly an opening. Upon Gaea's guidance, and without a sound, we hurried through the opening and were within the Sacred Grove at last.

Chapter Fifteen

༿

The Sacred Grove

Stone walls enclosed this Sacred Grove. All life within these walls was protected by a deity. I was so tired I just had to sit down, and nearly collapsed at Gaea's feet. She smiled at me, and understood my exhaustion. I closed my eyes and almost fell into a deep sleep, but my grandmother came over to me to hug me, and put her hand on my lower right calf.

"Dearest granddaughter, what happened to you?" my grandmother, Euterpe, asked, as she caressed my lower leg.

"I don't know. I didn't feel anything when we were walking. What is it? Does it look serious?" I answered unaware I had been deeply gashed.

"Don't worry, we will heal you. Nothing bad can happen to you here. We will stay as long as we can, as long as we are allowed," comforted my grandmother. "Lie down while I gather some herbs and sacred oils."

I rested my head on some gathered leaves. The splendor and beauty of the Sacred Grove were indescribable. I felt complete peace. I couldn't imagine another place more glorious in heaven or earth. I had heard about sacred groves, but couldn't believe I was actually in one. The air was sweet, the trees were a lush green, and I could see the dew resting on certain special leaves. The herbs were fragrant, and I knew secret herbal remedies lived within this Sacred Grove.

There were also extraordinary, vibrant crystals peeking out from their hiding places.

Gaea sat down beside me and told me of an ancient temple that was built in the Sacred Grove thousands of years ago. She promised to take me to it, but first, I had to rest for a while. She looked so happy and contented to be there, as if she was visiting an old friend she hadn't seen in a while.

Artemis greeted and visited her animals, as she was their protector and teacher. They loved her and were loyal to her, sharing secret information only with her. Eos meditated and exuded a luminous beauty only she could radiate.

I was fascinated by what was revealed to me, but felt a little overwhelmed by all the energy, the aromas, the beauty, the oxygen, and from my wound. My grandmother returned to my side with her arms full of greens and berries. From somewhere deep within the bag she carried, she pulled out a small bowl and a pestle. She sat down beside me and crushed the greens and berries. They released a fragrance I couldn't explain, but it relaxed and comforted me.

My grandmother smiled as she caressed my forehead and told me not to worry about anything. Then she spread the herbal mixture over my leg wound, and covered it with a large leaf. The leaf adhered to my leg, and my grandmother covered it with the fabric of my pants. My grandmother wiped the remaining oil from the ground herbs in her bowl with a piece of linen she carried, and tied it at both ends with a piece of vine. She then placed this medicinal and aromatic herb on my chest so I could inhale the soothing aromatherapy and rest.

"Sleep now, Calliope. There is time for your adventures, but now you must rest," my grandmother said to me.

I slept for what felt like days. When I awoke, the Sacred Grove was still in a state of eternal dawn. I never wanted to leave this enchanted place and secretly prayed I could stay there forever. At first I felt hazy, but as my eyes cleared, so did my head. I lifted my pant leg and the leaf. The herbal mixture had disappeared. My wound was completely healed!

My grandmother was always full of surprises but I had no idea she was such a gifted healer. I understood why she kept that gift veiled and was grateful for the healing she had given me. I sat up and looked around the Sacred Grove anxious to learn the lessons I was there to be taught. I was alone. My grandmother, Gaea, Eos, and Artemis had disappeared, yet I felt their spirits calling me.

I stood up and my curiosity pulled me forward. I wanted to explore every inch of the Sacred Grove, and took my first steps deeper into the forest. Birds were singing and flying happily overhead. Hummingbirds, bluebirds, doves, and birds I had never seen before welcomed me with their joyous song. Happily I continued my stroll, looking at everything my eyes and soul could ingest. I stopped to look at crystals, picked berries, and inhaled the fragrant greens and the lush aromas of purity. I found a brook to wash my face in and drank of its pure liquid, as I was dehydrated and couldn't drink enough water. I dipped my feet into the water and felt its energy surge up my body. A jolt of ki energy filled my entire being. My third eye burst with new vision.

I saw a vision of an ancient temple with massive columns and an open-air veranda. The temple floor was made of white marble and in the center was an enormous flame burning eternally. There were a few women there who seemed to be talking and teaching one another secrets of the universe. It was an ancient Mystery School!

I wanted to go to that temple and prayed to be led there. Through my intuition and vision, my elder women guardians, who were already there, called me to them. A majestic crystal then appeared before me on the ground. I picked it up and it tingled in my hand. The tip of it glowed as I held it in one direction. When I held it to my eyes to gaze into it, I saw images and prophetic scenes. I lowered my hand and the crystal, and as I held it in another direction it glowed even brighter, pulling me forward. I understood it meant to guide me to the ancient temple I had just seen in my vision. I knew my prayer had been answered. I was being led to the ancient Mystery School!

I was so excited, I could barely contain my spirit. All my life I had searched for a school I could train in and learn the ancient ways. I humbly and gratefully accepted the guidance and ran in the direction the crystal led. It was fun being led by the crystal. It seemed as excited as I was to be leading the way to the secret temple. It was like a honing bird accomplishing its mission, and proud of its work.

I always loved crystals and knew they held energy I didn't always understand. Some say that beings from another dimension can inhabit a crystal and make themselves known. To be the keeper of a crystal such as this was a great honor. Even if I were the keeper or student of this crystal for a brief time, I would honor it and never forget it.

I felt like I ran for miles before I came to a clearing in the Sacred Grove. I felt I should have an offering to leave at the temple doorway, and instinctively knew it should be the crystal.

Approaching the temple with great awe I stepped forward, mindfully placing each foot in front of the other while clearing my mind of distractions. I smelled incense. As I approached the temple I saw some women in walking meditation, and others talking quietly. I thought I saw my grandmother, but wasn't sure. As soon as I was at the threshold of the temple, the crystal indicated its work was finished and it seemed to go to sleep. I thanked it for its assistance and guidance, and prepared to leave it as an offering to the temple.

The great flame was before me and I saw other crystals lovingly placed there and felt that was where this crystal belonged. Filled with deep gratitude, I placed the crystal at the great flame. I searched for my grandmother. I felt something in my gut, turned around, and there she was . . . my beautiful grandmother!

"You have done well, my dear. We called you here and you answered. You are more developed than you think. I believe you are ready for higher-level training. You are in an incredibly sacred temple, my dear. It took me years to earn the right to be here. I was much older than you are today. There are ancient mysteries taught here, only to those who have proven themselves to be worthy. Come, let us walk. Let me show you some of my favorite places within this glorious temple," said my grandmother.

We walked around the temple gardens as my grandmother pointed out every plant, every flower, every crystal, and every secret. We sat by the great flame while my grandmother told me some of the ancient stories, revealing metaphysical truths and formulas for magic. Then Artemis joined us, and as she did, flying dolphins floated through the sky! How could they be flying, I wondered to myself.

I had seen the ancient Minoan frescoes on Crete and other places in Greece and ancient pottery with images of flying dolphins. Was it possible the ancient Minoans had been to this temple or one like it? Had the dolphins taught the ancient ones in the mystery schools of antiquity what they were about to teach me? It was all a dream, one that I didn't want to awaken from.

The Circle of Olympians

The dolphins circled around us and seemed to smile at us. Awestruck, I recognized them as the same dolphins that had protected me in the ocean when I swam with Amphitrite to Poseidon's temple. They followed me to the great temple within the Sacred Grove! How incredible! Had they been watching me the whole time? They were my guardians, teachers, and protectors, and they could fly! Then Amphitrite greeted me with all the warmth and love she had shepherded me with in the great ocean temple of Poseidon. She taught me so much, and to see her again was a thrill. What was about to happen, I wondered?

Gaea, Artemis, and Eos joined us, and we sat at the foot of the great flame. The dolphins continued to fly around us in the temple. My grandmother held out her scroll. It dawned on me that she was about to reveal the meaning of the scroll and the vision she had so long ago. The other women were silent yet present and would talk after my grandmother finished speaking.

Chapter Sixteen

Enemy Revealed

My grandmother unraveled the scroll as she cuddled closer to me. She read from the beginning of the scroll, the history of the ages that lived on its parchment. It spoke of creation, the beginning of the universe, the galaxies, and all sentient beings who dwelt within it. She read for hours and I was captivated by every moment, every breath, and every word. All the holy and sacred texts were mentioned. All faiths were revered and described in the scroll. All events in history were predicted . . . all wars and all events. Things that were predicted thousands of years ago had already happened. It was all written and we were simply playing out our destinies.

My grandmother then paused and prepared for the next chapter she was about to read. She looked deep into my soul to prepare me for the words about to be spoken. Then the words that would change my life reached my ears and my soul. My grandmother read our family name and the prophecy, which awaited our lineage! Some of the names she read I recognized, others I did not. I looked at her and the elder goddess women around me, sensing they knew what I was about to hear and learn.

My grandmother then read my name and the prophecy for my life. I almost fainted from the enormous task set before me. The prophecy was startlingly accurate up to that point in my life, so I knew the rest of the prophecy was bound to unfold. The scroll revealed everything I had been through in my life, including all the heartache and disappointments. Yet I learned those things happened so I could develop compassion for others, as I would one day help heal others through my writing.

My grandmother continued reading about my ancestors, and the heroic things they had done to protect our heritage, our lineage, the scroll, the amulet, and my destiny. She revealed future events I would experience and learn from, and tests that were yet to come. I had done well thus far, and proved myself worthy of the life written for me, but there was more to come, and a fierce enemy who would try to stop me. Of this enemy, my grandmother read from the scroll as well.

Gaea, Artemis, Eos, and Amphitrite then spoke of how they would help me and protect me, and the different skills each would teach me. Gaea vowed to teach me the secrets of the earth, and how to call upon her elements for help, protection, and inspiration when I needed them. Artemis promised to teach me more about hunting and defense, and the essential warrior skills she was expert at. Amphitrite would always be by my side in the water and help me call upon my dolphin friends for protection. Eos would teach me about the light, about the dawn and how to light my path before me. And my precious grandmother vowed to always protect me and to teach me the gift of vision.

Overwhelmed by these gracious gifts, I gave thanks to the Divine. I prayed to be worthy of such teachers and lessons. I touched my amulet, and caressed the scroll my grandmother had just read from. I had so many questions. Who wrote the scroll? Was it written by the hand of God? How did it come into my grandmother's possession? Did anyone else know about it? Was my enemy chasing me for the scroll as well? Did the keeper of the scroll and the amulet hold special powers evil ones wanted to possess?

My grandmother put the scroll down. Gaea, Artemis, Eos, and Amphitrite stood up and led me to a small sacred bath with a flowing fountain. They stepped into the bath and invited me to do the same. They washed their faces in preparation for prayers, and I did the same.

Artemis had gathered food and set it beside the altar we were about to approach. She was remarkable. She defended women at all costs, especially if they were threatened, yet wasn't swift to inflict her wrath. I was awed to be in her presence let alone be a student of hers. I was in awe to be the apprentice and ward of all these women and goddesses. Who would ever believe me if I dared to write about it?

We then stepped out of the bath fully clothed and wiped our feet dry. Together we walked to the great flame, in front of which was an altar dedicated to the Divine. My grandmother, who I was beginning to suspect was one of the Muses, then led us in song. She revealed herself as an enchantress. As my grandmother sung with her soul, the entire universe seemed to join her. Eos added her voice and her glorious dawn so that the light we were already bathed in became even brighter.

Gaea, the earth mother, joined in with her voice, and the earth seemed to exhale and open its Sacred Grove to us even more, becoming more fragrant with our song. Artemis and all her followers chimed in as the hummingbird shared its rainbows with our notes. Amphitrite and the dolphins joined our song, and added a golden light to the stream of water flowing beside the temple.

The Circle of Olympians

My grandmother led us in a song of prayer, devotion, and gratitude to the Divine. We sang for what felt like hours. The chant established an internal vibration within me I had never felt before. It transported me to another level of vision and bonded us together in a way that only music could. When it was time, my grandmother ended our singing, and indicated we should leave an offering to the Divine. Each one left something precious: incense, food, or a gift of gratitude. My grandmother picked up the scroll again and finished reading my destiny.

"Calliope," she whispered, "what I am about to read is the most sacred knowledge ever written. You must swear at this moment to hold the secrets I am about to reveal to you in your heart until your very last day on earth," she pleaded.

"Grandmother, I promise to keep this sacred knowledge deep within my heart and soul, but you must help me to do so," I begged.

"Of course, my darling," she promised. "All of us will help you. And there are others who will come to help you that you have not yet met. Calliope, this ancient scroll contains the secrets of the universe. Our family has been the guardian of it for thousands of years and we have guarded it well. The enemy and her family have been trying to steal it for as many years. We have had to become fierce warriors to defend the scroll. The amulet that you wear is a key to the scroll, and to the final portion of the scroll, which has yet to be written. The end of the scroll represents the end of times, which can either be apocalyptic or idyllic, the fate of which will be determined by the wearer of the amulet," my grandmother said.

I couldn't believe what my grandmother just read to me. It was too much. I was overwhelmed and wanted to refuse my destiny, which was written for my life. I was terrified. There was no way I could handle the responsibility placed on my shoulders. I felt faint and my vision became blurry. I couldn't hear clearly, and I was sure I had just lost my mind.

Everything that surrounded me was like a dream. If I had prayed the prayer of my life at that moment, it would have been to remain in the paradise of the Sacred Grove and the temple we were in. Yet I wasn't sure it was real any more. Maybe my imagination had gotten the best of me and I was simply lost, deep within a lucid dream. I comforted myself with that thought for just a moment, and then my grandmother took me by the shoulders and spoke deep into my heart.

"It is too late for you to back out of your destiny, Calliope," my grandmother cautioned. "It is not possible. I understand your feelings, because they are the same feelings I had when the scroll was first read to me and I was given the amulet to protect. And it was the same for your mother when I first read the scroll to her. But her identity, strength, knowledge, and power were concealed to protect you and her. Your mother is the vision keeper and your guardian. My precious granddaughter, don't you think I wanted out of this fate when I first learned of it? Don't you think I was scared at first, and still am at times?" she asked me.

"I don't know what to think, grandmother, but you're so much stronger than me, and much stronger than I will ever be," I cried.

"Calliope, age brings a certain strength youth could never know. The things that frighten you now frightened me when I was your age, but you will see that you are stronger than you think. You must fulfill your destiny. It is a great honor that God has chosen our family, and you are the one to fulfill the final chapter. The one who has the amulet and the scroll will write the final chapter for humankind. The end times will either be apocalyptic, with people destroying themselves and the earth, or they will realize at last that they can create a utopia on earth for all to share. Through your writing and vision, Calliope, you will write the final chapter, and through your storytelling, write the manifestation of utopia," said my grandmother.

I felt relieved. Writing was my sanctuary and dearest friend. Going deep into vision was joyous for me, so that was no problem. After I thought about it for a few moments, I felt more accepting of my destiny. After all, my ancestors had guarded the scroll and the amulet through several generations. They had protected me and raised me in a loving home. Now I only had to write the final chapter to determine the fate of humankind. I could easily do that in the sanctuary and protection of the Sacred Grove. I breathed a huge sigh of relief when my grandmother looked at me and continued.

"There is one final thing to be aware of, Calliope, and that is your enemy, Medusa. She is a Gorgon, a tribe of warlike women. If she steals the amulet and scroll, then she will have the power to write the final chapter and the outcome of the end times. She would write a chapter so full of annihilation the world would be destroyed. There would be no second chance, nor anywhere else for humanity to go should she take possession of these priceless and potent keys to eternity. She will hunt you as you have never been hunted before. She, too, has been training all her life. And generations of her family have been training for centuries in the ways of the wicked through sorcery, trickery, cloaking, deception, poison making, and dark spell casting.

"Long ago," my grandmother continued, "the ancient elders of her family were good and pure. Our families were once close and deeply bonded. It is said deep in our family lore that both families were given the task of protecting the God-given scroll and amulet. The matriarch of their family was a pure soul, full of light and love for the world. For generations our families lived in harmony, protecting the scroll and amulet. But as God wrote the scroll, the outcome became clearer. Our family was chosen as the tribe to guard the amulet and scroll until the end times. The evil family then became consumed with jealousy and grew determined to steal them back.

"Once they knew the true power of the scroll and the amulet, they couldn't live without them or the joint power they held," my grandmother warned. "Each subsequent generation became more consumed with greed and power, and wanted to control the world. It is believed they became evil, and the legend says their children married into evil families, planting the seed for your current enemy. Yet God has been good to us. He has protected us and taught us the ways to thwart their evil. He has remained one step ahead of them at all times, and has trained us well. He will do the same for you, Calliope.

"You already know an evil spirit has been tracking you, trying to steal the amulet and get the scroll. But what you have not known is that she is someone you already know. She is your half sister!" my grandmother proclaimed.

Chapter Seventeen

Victorious Vow

  I was stunned, but something deep within my soul was hit. Somehow I knew this was true. I thought for a moment about all the wicked things my half sister did to my family and I over the years. All her cruelty suddenly made sense to me. I understood why my family believed she robbed the family fortune and me of my inheritance and stole my most prized possessions and gifts of antiquity my grandmother gave my mother as a wedding gift, and why they believed she ultimately killed my father in his weakest days.

  Her malice made sense. She was trying to break me because she knew of my destiny before I did. If my half sister couldn't completely destroy me, she thought she could weaken me to the point where I would wearily reveal where the amulet and scroll were hidden. What she failed to understand was that I wasn't as stupid as she thought, nor were my mother and grandmother.

  In that moment, all fear, doubt, and insecurity left me. I knew I could take her in a fight, and that I would avenge the evil she had visited upon my family. In the next moment, I became a fierce warrior, determined to be undefeated in my life and destiny. Revealing my half sister's identity was the most empowering thing my grandmother did for me because it gave meaning to the suffering my half sister caused in my life. And where meaning could be brought forth from suffering, the suffering was not in vain. I was committed to victory!

Studying me, my grandmother said, "Well done, Calliope. I can see it all makes sense to you. You are not afraid anymore. But do not allow your anger to make you believe in false powers. Remember, you are human. You must not become over confident, for you will be most vulnerable when you believe you are indestructible."

I listened carefully to my grandmother and adjusted my frame of mind accordingly, remaining confident, but cautious. Now that I knew who my enemy was, I remembered the shark deep in Poseidon's sea, and the depth of dark energy I felt with it. I believed that my half sister was much more evil than I had ever imagined.

"Do not wish for the blood of another on your sword, for the blood you find on the blade may be your own. Remember this, Calliope," my grandmother warned. "Still it is good that you know who she is, and what she is after. Finally, you have come into your power. This was essential before you could complete your mission. Yet, Calliope, there is one more element you will need before you fulfill your destiny and write the final chapter for the world. You must find the pen of the Divine, which is on the island of Delos. You will have to go there to retrieve the pen. Then you will be able to write the final chapter of the ancient scroll.

"This journey will be the most dangerous of your life, for your half sister and her evil spirit and its many manifestations will be chasing you," my grandmother warned. "We will protect you, but you must finish your training with a few more crucial skills. For now, it is time to celebrate and give thanks to God for His love and protection. We must also rest,

The Circle of Olympians

for the time is fast approaching when we must go to Delos to retrieve the pen. Time is running out for the world. We must not fail to save it."

I absorbed every word she spoke. I trusted her wisdom, God's love and protection, and the shelter and love of the goddesses I was entrusted to. I also had to trust myself and my training. All my life I had been training and preparing, but I didn't know for what until now. Now I knew. I vowed to train even harder both physically and metaphysically. But for now, it was time to celebrate.

My grandmother, Gaea, Eos, Artemis, Amphitrite, and I danced together, and laughed, ate, and drank the nectar of the gods. I said a prayer of thanks to God, and asked Him to guide me through my journey and help me fulfill my destiny. I then rested more deeply than I ever had before in my life. I had so much to contemplate, so much on my shoulders, but I wasn't alone with the burden. I would soon learn that the Divine had heard my prayers and answered them abundantly.

Chapter Eighteen

༄

Journey to Delos

Eos brought in the dawn and gently awoke all of us. Reluctantly, I opened my eyes and for that special first moment of the day, all I knew was bliss. Then I remembered what happened the day before and everything I learned. The weight of my destiny was upon my soul, and although I was nervous, I knew I was going to succeed.

Gaea walked towards me. "Calliope, we have consulted the Divine. It is time for your journey to Delos to find the Divine pen. Your grandmother and I have discussed your half sister. We know her as Medusa. We may need to separate to throw her off your scent. We have devised a plan," Gaea said.

"No, I don't want us to split up! I want to stay together! I want to go to Delos together. I need all of you with me to find the pen and succeed," I pleaded.

My grandmother came to my side and stroked my back with her healing hand. "Sweetheart, don't worry. Everything will be all right. We prayed with all our heart and asked God to guide us in our decision. We looked into the future and have seen that Medusa is already aware of your progress. She knows you are close to fulfilling your destiny, but is not exactly sure where you are or what your next step will be. However, she is a very gifted seer and it won't take her long to figure out what your next step will be. I,

The Circle of Olympians

however, am a better seer than she. I have seen that she will consult the oracle at Delphi for her answers. She is foolish enough to think that the oracle will speak to her and guide her, but I have devised a plan. It will throw her off your scent, at least for a while. I will go to Delphi, pretend to be the oracle, and give her false instructions that will lead her far away from you. If she forces me, I may finish her off for good," my grandmother declared.

"No!" I screamed. "You mustn't do this, grandmother! I don't want anything to happen to you. I will not allow you to do it!" I cried.

"You must not worry, my darling," my grandmother comforted. "This is something I feel I must do for you. I have met Medusa many times, and have always been victorious. Yet I will heed my own warning and remember I am not invincible. And Calliope, I will not go alone," my grandmother said as she opened her arm to the garden to reveal another surprise.

I looked toward the garden area of the temple grounds within the Sacred Garden and couldn't believe my eyes. It was Uncle George! How did he get here? What was he doing here? I thought only women and goddesses were allowed within this sacred forest, but I was overjoyed to see him. He looked a little different to me as I ran to embrace him.

"Uncle George, I'm so happy to see you. You have no idea what I have been going through and what I have learned. You'll never believe what grandma told me," I said to him, almost out of breath.

He said nothing but smiled the deep, all knowing expression he offered that housed a thousand words . . . the smile my family always cherished in him. It dawned on me that he knew for many years everything I recently learned, and he was about to reveal his own secrets to me. I looked at him closer and noticed that his shoes had small wings. In his hand he carried his hat, which also had wings on it. I never noticed wings on his hat or shoes, but that day, the wings were as clear as day to me.

Uncle George, the gentle saint of our family, had always been the steady rock in the lives of my mother and grandmother, ever since my grandfather passed away many years ago. He was the rock of my family. He never said an unkind word and was very shy. His words were few but potent, and his sense of humor was charming and always sweet. He walked with a slight limp and took his time in life, as he did with his step. That he suddenly appeared in the Sacred Grove with winged shoes and a winged hat stunned me. It gave me cause to wonder who he really was. He looked at me with a spark in his eye, and waved to my grandmother who soon joined us. They hugged one another, and both smiled at me.

"You see, Calliope, I won't be alone. Uncle George will be with me and make sure I will be safe," my grandmother assured me.

Uncle George looked at me and put his arm around me. "Don't worry, Calliope. I will take good care of your grandmother. I promise not to let anything happen to her. I also promise to let you know how we're doing along the way," Uncle George said to me as he revealed a magic wand he carried in his hand.

"Uncle George, what is that?" I asked.

"It is my magic wand," he replied. "There are many things I can do with this wand, like communicate anything I want to whomever I choose, whenever I want. Although my walk is slow, I will now reveal the truth to you, Calliope, of my real speed and my true identity. You see, I am the messenger of the gods . . . the fastest one among them. As part of your family, I was chosen to help you and your grandmother. That is why I have come to you now."

It dawned on me who he really was . . . Hermes, the messenger! Now, I realized why Uncle George said

The Circle of Olympians

so little most of the time. He had protected his true identity and by saying little, he learned everything. He could best serve his role as messenger by saying little so that when he spoke others would truly listen. Plus, that he usually walked with a limp, he hid his true speed. Ingenious! Now I finally understood why he always played music in the house, loved the stars and knew so much about them, and especially cared for the olive trees around the Ithacan family home, and pressed his own olive oil. Everything I knew about Hermes, I suddenly saw in Uncle George.

I breathed deeply and centered myself, trying to handle everything that unraveled before me. I tried to see if I felt all right about my grandmother and Uncle George leaving for Delphi to thwart Medusa off my track. Even though they wouldn't listen to me because they were determined to protect me, my gut instinct was worth exploring. I prayed to God for His guidance and closed my eyes to listen to my heart for His answer. When I opened my eyes, Uncle George and my grandmother were looking deep into my eyes. They assured me they would be all right.

"Calliope, it is time for us to go," my grandmother said.

I hugged her with my soul and embraced Uncle George, too. I asked them to swear a solemn vow that they would return unharmed. They both swore that they would. I sobbed as they left the Sacred Grove, and wasn't sure I could handle the separation. Then Gaea came to comfort me, and Eos added her love and light. Both held me and comforted me, until my spirit finally calmed.

"They will be all right, Calliope," promised Artemis. "I have charged my animals to protect them. I will guard them and make sure nothing happens to them. They will not be alone, for they are too valuable to God. It is time for us to go. Time will not wait for us."

Gaea said, "We must gather our belongings and initiate our journey, as the moon is full. There is another who is on his way to help us, Calliope. We will meet him at the appropriate time. Gather your things, eat this fruit, and let us go," Gaea instructed me.

Gaea cleared the temple area where we had celebrated, ate, and sang the night before. And she placed the ancient scroll safely away, where no evil spirit could find it. At that moment, Gaea, Eos, Artemis, Amphitrite, and I walked out of the Sacred Grove and journeyed far to the edge of the Mediterranean.

Chapter Nineteen

Apollo

Exhausted, I begged to rest and Gaea gave her permission. We were at the foot of the Mediterranean. I dangled my feet over the rock I was sitting on to touch the liquid crystal. The sun called me into a trance. I had no choice but to follow, and closed my eyes for a while.

When I opened my eyes, I stared at the mountains that were beyond the horizon. Hazily at first, but then very clearly, a chariot, carrying the sun behind it, led by four white horses, blazed across the sky. The driver barreled towards me, storming through the fire of the sun, but I was not afraid. I realized it was Apollo. He quickly rode closer and told me to get into the chariot. I looked at Artemis, Apollo's twin sister, for guidance. She nodded her permission for me to go. He was the additional help Gaea spoke of.

Apollo, the god of music, played a golden lyre. He was also the archer and god of healing who taught man medicine, and was fed ambrosia and sacred nectar. Each morning, Apollo drove the sun across the sky in his chariot.

I took a deep breath and stepped into his chariot, holding on tightly to the side of the chariot as we rode at a speed I had never known. We rode towards the horizon, towards the place where Time ends.

"Calliope, I have come to help you and to see to it that you fulfill your destiny," Apollo told me. "The gods have invested much in humanity, and we want to see your race continue through eternity. We do not want you to annihilate yourselves. You are the hope for the world right now. I will teach you about truth, healing, and prophecy."

As we continued driving in his chariot, carrying the sun across the horizon, a small island made of rock appeared . . . Delos, Apollo's birthplace. In ancient Greece, Delos had been the cultural and religious center for a thousand years.

We followed the magnificent Sacred Way that led to the remains of the Sanctuary of Apollo. We aimed for the center of Delos. As it seemed we were about to crash into it, the island opened to welcome us. We rode to a sacred spot deep within one of Delos' rocky mountains. Apollo jumped off the chariot and ran to a holy fire burning in the center of the secret cave, deep within the mountain. He scooped up a small handful of flames, but was not burned. He invited me to sit down and watch the flames with him. I sat down and stared into the flames, feeling lonely without my grandmother. I was worried about her, and wished I were with Gaea, Artemis, Eos, and Amphitrite.

"Don't be afraid, Calliope," Apollo said. "Don't worry about your grandmother and Uncle George. I promise they will be all right. I am here to help you. I will teach you many things, but we do not have much time."

As I listened to him, I noticed that the smoke from the great fire was traveling up towards an almost invisible opening in the mountain. I wondered where this opening led, and later learned that while we were on the island of Delos, we were also somehow beneath the oracle at Delphi.

All the legends were true. That was why the temple at Delphi was dedicated to Apollo, because his sacred and secret home was beneath it. His flames traveled up towards the oracle to infuse the priestess with the gift of prophecy. I couldn't believe what was being revealed to me on this journey. The world would never believe me if I ever dared to write about it!

Then Apollo revealed the sacred scroll, sealed again with a sacred seal. He told me I could read it whenever I wanted to within this secret cave by the sacred fire.

I removed the seal and asked him if I could keep it. Apollo said yes and I put it in my medicine pouch. I unrolled the parchment but could make out only a few words. I read as much as I could before my tired eyes wore out. In my hands, I held the secrets of the universe, yet I could not take them with me. Would I remember the sacred secrets, or would they vanish from my memory once I left the belly of the mountain? I did not know, but prayed to remember everything.

"As you walk this path, a new secret will be revealed to you," said Apollo. "There is a finite set of laws which rule the universe. None can be broken. Obeying all brings harmony. God wrote them all a long time ago, yet time cannot change or destroy them. Time is His instrument to bring about that which He has written.

"You will be able to read all the laws when you finish your journey and have fulfilled your destiny. Then it will be up to you to share what you have learned with others, yet keep secret what is meant to be hidden," Apollo continued.

As I stared at the scroll, specifically the section that spoke of the secrets of the universe, the text of the first secret became very clear.

I read the scroll: "I am the center of the universe, the Creator of all things visible and invisible. My children are the wise and the free, and the lovers of all that is good. You, dear reader, fill the distance between my heart and soul. And I am the Spirit that guides you, and moves you to endure all things."

The rest of the text became invisible for a moment, as if to guide me to meditate on this first revelation. I realized we were all God's children and the center of His universe. The scroll wasn't speaking about me only but about all who read it. The scroll revealed God's love for us, for the gods, and for the Olympians who had been charged with protecting the scroll, as well as God's heart. They were supposed to help humankind love one another and God. That they sometimes tested us was only to strengthen us.

I looked at Apollo. We sat by the sacred fire together and meditated for a while. I prayed to God to protect my grandmother and Uncle George. I asked for a sign that they were all right. Miraculously, Uncle George suddenly appeared by the fire and hugged me.

"Calliope, we are all right. Don't worry. Your grandmother is a strong and fierce woman. Nothing will happen to her," Uncle George promised. "We are right above you, and your grandmother will orchestrate everything to manipulate Medusa. If the right opportunity presents itself, we will stop her forever, rid the universe of her evil, and avenge our family."

Upon the surface of a smooth rock, Uncle George showed me, as if we were looking at a movie screen, that he and my grandmother were safely disguised and hidden. They were resting, waiting for Medusa to fall into the trap they had set for her. My nerves were calmed and my anxiety lessened.

"I will be back soon, Calliope, but I must return to your grandmother's side to protect her," Uncle George promised as he hugged me again.

I hugged Uncle George with all my heart and felt comforted that he and my grandmother were so close. I looked at Apollo and could tell there was much more he wanted to teach me.

The Circle of Olympians

"Calliope, let us take a walk. There are many things I want to show you and teach you," Apollo said to me as he picked up his silver bow and golden lyre.

I secured my backpack, made sure my medicine pouch and amulet were securely around my neck, and braced myself. We walked out of Apollo's secret cave, and came out into a clearing of sand and rock. We were alone, yet I felt we were being watched. First we walked to the heights of the highest peak on Delos to view the panoramic view of the island. Apollo revealed many secrets of the universe to me, as well as secrets of his island birthplace, of healing, of poetry, of prophecy, and of the fate of humankind.

Off in the distance, he showed me his dolphins. He revealed that he could express himself in dolphin form... Delphinus, and told me that they were revered at Delphi. It was all coming together in my mind. The threads of eternity were weaving a tapestry I was somehow an essential part of. Where it would end I couldn't possibly know, but I had to remain present every moment to absorb each lesson of every minute I was blessed to receive.

Apollo began to play intoxicating music on his lyre that lifted my soul to another dimension. My vision grew deeper as he continued to play. I perceived events of antiquity: all wars and battles for land and honor, all famines, all empires, and all the brilliant artistic and philosophical developments of the ancient Greek civilization. I also understood the role of women of antiquity. I knew they were more powerful than the world was led to believe.

As Apollo continued to play on his lyre, my vision became deeper and more intense. I had always been blessed with the gift of vision, but Apollo's music and the island sanctuary amplified my vision to another level and another dimension. It led up to the present day and I perceived all the crises around the world. I saw each country and the suffering its people were enduring. I saw all diseases, all poverty and famine, and all misery and pain.

Joy was still on the earth, but it was vanishing at a rapid rate. Humankind was turning against one another, and against the earth itself. People had lost their way. They stopped caring for Mother Earth who had always taken such good care of them. It didn't make sense to me, but seeing things from a global point of view put into perspective for me the dire need for humanity to act now to save the earth and one another.

Humanity was at a turning point. The outcome depended on the final chapter of the ancient scroll. That I was to finish writing the ancient scroll, with the help of God and the Olympians, was still more than I could comprehend, but I was determined to succeed. I opened my eyes for a moment, and wanted to make notes in my journal, but Apollo stopped me. He told me my vision must remain unwritten until I wrote the final chapter of the scroll, to ensure the safety of the final outcome of the end times, and to protect humanity and myself. He continued to play the lyre and I closed my eyes again, allowing myself to be lulled into the future.

My vision of the future presented one of two possible outcomes. The first vision became very clear, as I saw a panoramic view of the entire world. I saw an idyllic world, a utopian paradise, filled with peace and harmony and a natural beauty unmatched by anything I had ever seen. The green of the trees was lush beyond any emerald imaginable. The waters of the oceans, lakes, rivers, streams, and waterfalls were crystalline and prismatic. The flowers were abundant and radiant, and the colors I saw were beyond any rainbow my eyes had ever seen.

Most beautifully, the people of the world were living in harmony, being loving and compassionate to one another, sharing their goods, and helping one another. The animals were loved and cared for, and so was the earth, the gentle Mother. The animals of the seas were cared for and protected because humanity was sheltering the precious waters of the earth.

I felt a peace in this vision unlike any other I had ever felt in my life. It dawned on me that it was possible to bring about Heaven on earth. Perhaps that was what all creation had been leading up to. It was a world so beautiful, so enchanting. Nothing bad would ever happen in a world so filled with love and grace.

In this angelic world, there were no more diseases, poverty, hatred, or jealousy, and no more greed. Humanity learned that sharing and caring for one another was the way to live. How they reached that outcome I wasn't sure, but I tried to absorb and remember everything I saw in this vision.

Apollo then stopped playing his lyre and gently woke me from my vision. He looked at me and said, "Calliope, there could also be another outcome to the end times."

He began to play again but the notes were somber and grim, and led me into another vision . . . a horrible final chapter of the scroll and end times. Deeper and deeper I went into vision. I felt cold. Around me was an unending darkness I couldn't describe. There was no end to the darkness and the negativity it held. All the sins of humanity lived within this murkiness. I prayed for protection and invisibility for I knew I was in dangerous territory.

In this second vision of mine, the world had been destroyed. All hope was gone, humanity was decimated, and those who remained struggled against a slow death. Nature herself was destroyed. The trees had vanished, the waters were polluted, most of the animals had died, and disease was rampant. There were no longer any hospitals for people to go to. Everything was in scarce supply. Everyone hoarded whatever scraps they had. People killed one another for water.

Evil had captured humanity's soul and was choking it to death. By that point, it was too late. God's heart was broken. Nothing was left. The plan, the creation, the undying, eternal, unconditional love had all been for nothing, because humanity betrayed God and the Divine nature living within them. Humanity had betrayed itself.

It was too much for me to absorb. I wanted to know how this had happened. I knew Medusa must have orchestrated this dreadful outcome. I had to know exactly how so that I could stop her, if my grandmother and Uncle George hadn't already done so at Delphi. I focused my attention on her, and asked God to show me the answers I was seeking.

Then I saw her. Her ugly image came into clearer view, first as a little girl. It seemed she was born evil, but became more wicked. As she grew older, it appeared she took pleasure in hurting others. She desperately wanted the scroll and amulet to write a horrible outcome for humanity. She believed her family would then be in control of the end times and therefore the world.

Because God had given humanity free choice, there wasn't much He could do to stop their choices, but He gave me the opportunity to alter humanity's fate for the better.

I couldn't fail. Medusa orchestrated her entire life to destroy me, to acquire the precious scroll and amulet. She cloaked her evil well, opening the door to the darkness. I knew what she was at my first sight of her, and for this, she always hated me. Her hatred for me would be eternal, especially because I was strong and would stop at nothing to defeat her.

Recently, she was training with her teachers and mastering dark, occult skills. But I was not afraid for God was on my side, and the Olympians trained me

The Circle of Olympians

in the ways of the ancients. I knew I would defeat her, but she would fight bitterly until the end.

My vision revealed that her final attempt to steal the scroll and amulet was about to happen. If she took possession of them, she would then be able to write the final chapter of the ancient scroll and determine the outcome of the end times and humanity. She was crafty enough to realize that if she got one of these precious items, the other would be near.

My vision continued to reveal that Medusa was traveling to Delphi to consult the oracle about my whereabouts. My grandmother and Uncle George were already there. My grandmother would provide her with answers as if she was the oracle, to throw Medusa off my track, sending her back to the United States. This would give me enough time to find the Divine pen and finish writing the last chapter. Then Apollo stopped playing his lyre and I opened my eyes. Startled by what I had just seen in my vision, I looked at him for help.

"There isn't much time, Calliope. We must hurry and find the Divine pen so you can write the final and magnificent chapter of the ancient scroll . . . what was revealed to you in vision," Apollo said.

"Where is the Divine pen, Apollo? Do you know?" I asked.

"Yes, but to prove the purity of your intention, you must find it on your own," Apollo instructed.

I thought I was home free. I believed I had been through the toughest part of the tests, and all I had to do was write the final chapter, which would have been easy for me. That I had to find the Divine pen, while I was worn out and worried about my grandmother and Uncle George, was the last straw.

"Please help me, Apollo! Tell me where the pen is so that I can write the final chapter and be done with it. If we are running out of time, isn't it better for you to tell me where it is so we don't take any chances with the final outcome of humanity and the world?" I pleaded.

"Calliope, you must trust yourself. I wish I could help you, but it was written long ago that you had to do this by yourself. It was written this way as a last defense for humanity that the writer of the final chapter was truly worthy of such a daunting task. Remember that you will have help and are never truly alone. You are stronger than you think. You can do this, Calliope. I promise you, you can do this. You must!" Apollo assured.

I wasn't so sure. I felt that, with time, I might have a chance of finding the Divine pen, but I wasn't too good under pressure. I had no choice, but didn't know where to begin looking for it.

"Here, Calliope. Have some ambrosia and nectar," Apollo said as he handed me a bowl of the food and a chalice of the drink . . . the food of the gods.

"Is it really all right for me to have this?" I asked.

"Yes it is, but don't have too much because you will then become immortal," Apollo cautioned.

To me, that wasn't such a bad outcome, but by then I learned things weren't as they always appeared. I decided to eat in moderation. I felt a delirious feeling of bliss and energy sweep over me. My mind could barely fathom that I was eating ambrosia, the ancient mix of barley, olive oil, cheese, fruit, and honey, and the sweet honeyed nectar. In antiquity, mortals were punished for trying to eat and drink this food of the gods, and there I was eating and drinking both without punishment.

Apollo began to play his lyre again to encourage me, and miraculously, the Muses responded to his music with theirs. As soon as the Muses appeared, I heard sounds of a waterfall. I was stunned! Could this be the Pierian Spring from Greek mythology where the Muses dip into the waters of inspiration

The Circle of Olympians

and allow artists and musicians and authors to drink of the water?

I was lulled into a divine trance. I was suddenly transported to another vision, hypnotized by the divine music being played for me. Then Artemis whispered in my ear, but I couldn't understand what she was trying to tell me. I settled into my center, breathed deeply, and tried to let my consciousness go while retaining part of my senses in order to hear her instruction.

"Fret not for I am with you, Calliope. Remember the promises we made to you. While you must fulfill your destiny alone, we will help you, guide you, and instruct you, if you implement what you learned during these last few weeks of training with us," Artemis said.

I wasn't sure where she was, or where Gaea, Amphitrite, and Eos were either, but I trusted they were with me in spirit.

"Go now to the temple dedicated to me on this island," Artemis instructed. "Go there as fast as you can and I will guide you once you are there. You must use all your intuition to find the Divine pen. Only you can find it and write the final chapter. Know how important you are Calliope, and that you are protected and you will not be afraid."

I gathered my journal and backpack. I checked the amulet once more making sure my medicine pouch was securely around my neck. I made sure I still had the bow and arrows Artemis gave me in the Sacred Grove for I knew anything could happen on my adventure. I looked at Apollo for encouragement. Then I tied my shoes extra tight, and ran from the mountain peak I had been meditating on.

Chapter Twenty

Battle with Medusa

I felt the wind on my back and could hear the enchanting song of the Muses through the air. I was still in a mythic trance but I wasn't delusional. I ran down the hill keeping my focus and intention on finding the Temple of Artemis. I held the image in my mind of what I thought the temple would look like, as well as the image of what I thought the Divine pen would look like. I learned that energy followed intention and attention, and that whatever I focused my thoughts on would manifest, so it was time I put that into practice.

I was out of breath but had to keep running as fast as I could. Then I felt a cool breeze on my back and felt a chill deep within my soul. A notion of worry flashed across my mind about the safety of my grandmother and Uncle George. I stopped for a moment to ask Artemis if they were all right and she insisted I continue running.

"I need to know they are all right," I pleaded as I ran.

"They are safe, Calliope. Remember, they are not alone either, and have the Lord's protection with them. He will not allow anything to happen to them," she comforted. "You must carry on!" Artemis commanded.

The Circle of Olympians

I ran as fast as I could, unsure of where I was going but I was guided as each foot met the ground. I let go of trying to control the situation and tried to free my mind of worry and anxiety. I had to surrender to the situation at hand, and accept that I didn't know how things were going to end. I had to trust God, the Olympians, my higher self, and my training. I kept going and allowed my heart to lead the way.

Suddenly a clearing appeared before me and there it was . . . the Temple of Artemis! I was on hallowed ground even though only the remains of the temple were visible at first. My vision unexpectedly became unfocused, and the temple as it once was, in its pristine form, took shape before me. It was glorious, enchanting, and luminous. The great temple was filled with Divine light and peace. I was struck by its beauty and was momentarily frozen. Then Artemis appeared. She was visible but didn't say a word. I could still hear the music of the Muses, but it was faint. Artemis seemed to invite me to her, providing a clue as to where the Divine pen was hidden.

Then out of nowhere an evil spirit appeared, trying to prevent the completion of my mission. In a way I expected her, but was determined not to be defeated. I was fighting for something much greater than myself. I was fighting for the universe, for humanity and world peace, for the victory of the Light over evil. This fight I was not about to lose.

I clutched my amulet and made sure it was hidden. She . . . Medusa . . . had been after it all this time. I wasn't about to let her have it now. I said a prayer and asked for protection, centered my self and my power with my breath, and called upon all the help I could. This was my final test!

She was filled with venom and hatred, and all of it was focused on me. If she could stop me, she would control the world and its future. I was not about to let that happen. Even though I was scared, I was indomitably determined to win.

I drew my sword from its sheath. It released a chime that rang so loud it hurt her ears. For a moment her flight was halted, giving me enough time to cloak myself from her vision. Furious, she screamed at me, hoping I would reveal my place by my voice and my fear. I remained silent. She threw an evil cloud of smoke at me, hoping it would encase my form so she could direct her strike. Seeing it form from her belly, my breath engulfed hers, suffocating her with her own venom, and stopping her attack before it could even reach me.

There was no time for fear. I formed a cloud of translucent light around me to obscure Medusa's vision. I could still see Artemis, so I wasn't completely alone or in total danger. I could still hear the music of the Muses and Apollo's lyre, so I knew they were with me, too. I wondered what Medusa was doing at Artemis' temple? Had my grandmother and Uncle George not been able to defeat her or divert her? I was confused, but couldn't focus energy on my confusion. I had to reach Artemis because somewhere hidden near where she was standing was the Divine pen. That was why Medusa suddenly appeared.

I caught my breath. I breathed deeply but silently. How was I supposed to defeat Medusa? I hadn't completed my training, but had to call forth from the depths of my being all that I had to fight with. Surely this was the fight of my life and the fight for humanity. Silently I prayed to God, and called out to my elders for help and protection. I stood very still and watched her, as she would have liked to watch me.

Medusa was filled with fury and rage. She was ugly in a way I couldn't describe. Her internal darkness permeated the rest of her being. She was a tortured soul. Part of me felt compassion for her, but

I knew I had to keep my guard up. She was crafty in a way I was not, but I trusted God would protect me.

Medusa sensed Artemis, but I don't think she could see her. Medusa seemed to know she was close to the Divine pen. If I moved, she would sense me. If I didn't move, she would sooner or later find the Divine pen. I couldn't allow that. I prayed for guidance and waited for my answer.

It felt like an eternity before I heard the whisper of my grandmother, instructing me to remember my training and that I wasn't alone. I called upon the animals present for their help, and to my rescue they came. Medusa was also a fierce warrior who fought hard, calling upon her own beasts for help, and to fight those that had come to my defense.

My grandmother reminded me how I learned to confuse an enemy by manipulating her mind. I remembered and tried to do the technique. I hadn't practiced it very much but knew I could confuse Medusa, at least for a short time. She knew I was there, in the garden of the Temple of Artemis. She was furious for she couldn't see me. Thank God I was still wearing the amulet.

Then, she did something I had never seen before. She manifested a purple gray cloud and propelled it in my direction. It smelled foul and I gasped for breath, giving away my location. Immediately, she lunged at me. Before I knew what happened, she was on my throat. I could barely breathe.

"Calliope!" my grandmother screamed. "Remember your training!"

I tucked my head and chin down and turned to one side so that I could breathe. I managed to catch a bit of breath. I had never been held in such a tight chokehold. I felt completely immobilized and terrified, but couldn't give into my terror for the fight would have ended in an instant.

"Calliope, you must remember who you are!" cried my grandmother.

"We are with you, Calliope. Fight! Fight as hard as you have ever fought in your life! Do not give up," cried Gaea, from where I do not know.

Power ignited in me and surged all the way up my body, through every chakra and hit my inner eye. I was no longer afraid and cried my deepest kiai, gathering all my strength from the corners of the universe. I declared I would not be defeated and claimed my victory. I began to fight as the fierce warrior I had been trained to become.

I lowered to my knees and grabbed Medusa around the waist. I held onto her with all my strength. I threw her over my shoulder using my center and my spirit. She fell with a great thud. The ground and temple columns shook, but I was free and she was down.

Medusa looked at me with such a malevolent intent, I couldn't return her gaze. I remembered my Aikido training, and knew not to look into the enemy's eyes, for if I did, she would win my spirit. I looked at her but not into her. I forgot how much I hated her, how much pain she caused my family, and how happy I would be to avenge my family honor. It would be my pleasure to defeat her and to save humanity at the same time.

I knew I couldn't focus on my anger for that in itself would have defeated me. I tried to strengthen my compassion for her, as my adrenaline raced through my veins. I tried to bless her, and to think of her as a child. At that very moment, she stood up and spat poisonous venom at me. Part of it hit me and for a second I felt weak, as if I were about to pass out.

"Calliope, you must not inhale or rub your eyes!" screamed my grandmother. "Go to the herb tree behind you quickly and pick a leaf. Break it up and

The Circle of Olympians

rub it onto your skin and rub some of the oil into your eyes. Hurry!" she yelled.

Eos ignited a small bush steps from the Temple. I understood this was the bush I should break the leaves from, but Medusa tried to stop me. She tripped me and grabbed my leg. I could just about reach the small tree and begged for divine intervention. One of the animals came to my rescue and brought me a small leaf, as Medusa held my leg in a vice grip.

I did as my grandmother said and somehow managed to break Medusa's grip with a strong thrust of my hip and legs. I rolled away from her until I could do as my grandmother instructed. Hastily, I rubbed the broken leaves on my skin and the oil gently into my eyes. I regained full consciousness, and was relieved and grateful for the help.

I had to reach Artemis and the Divine pen before Medusa, but had to fight her off before I could do so. Otherwise I would reveal the location of the Divine pen. What was I supposed to do? Then Uncle George spoke to me.

"Calliope, use your bow," he commanded. "Aim for Medusa's heart."

Miraculously, the bow Artemis gave me was still on my back. I was a distance away from Medusa. If I could just load an arrow, I could take her out. I reached back for an arrow and was devastated to find none.

"Uncle George, help! Grandmother! Artemis! Help me! Gaea, hear my plea!" I begged.

Amazingly, under a bush and beside a rock, I saw a silver arrow. Medusa followed my gaze as we both raced for the arrow. I got my hands on it first and I continued to run deep into the bush beside the Temple of Artemis. She followed but wasn't as quick as I was. My training served me well.

"Help me!" I begged God.

Just as I was sure I couldn't load my arrow, the dolphins appeared flying in the sky. They lifted me up and took me away from Medusa, so that I could load my bow. She was furious but I was rescued and focused. As we flew in the air, close to the ground, I loaded my bow and centered on her with all my might. I poured my ki energy through my body, through my hand into the arrow. I drew the bow back. As I was about to release it, I offered a prayer of thanks, knowing the path of the warrior was one filled with gratitude. Just then, she disappeared.

The dolphins continued to carry me through the sky. I asked Eos to light the way so I could see where Medusa was. My grandmother then reminded me of my gift of vision. While still in the sky, I closed my eyes to truly see what was going on. Medusa was trying to lure me and set a trap, but I wasn't going to fall for it. I centered myself and knew God was on my side. Then my grandmother's voice instructed me to rush for the Temple doorway beside Artemis. I did as she said and asked the dolphins to escort me. As I was about to land, Medusa appeared at the door. My reflexes were quick. I drew the bow and aimed for her heart before she could settle herself into the ground. It struck her straight on and she collapsed to the ground. I looked at her in disbelief, but knew I had no time to lose.

"Hurry, Calliope, hurry!" my grandmother commanded.

I did as she said and looked at Artemis, who indicated where I would find the Divine pen. I entered the Temple and saw an illuminated marble box set upon an altar. Was it this obvious, I wondered? My grandmother answered my thought.

"Granddaughter, it is only obvious to you because God allowed you to see this. This vision and this box are not visible to everyone, but you must now fulfill your destiny and take hold of the pen," she said.

I was on hallowed ground. I ran towards the holy box, and knelt in gratitude offering a prayer of thanks. In awe, I lifted the heavy lid of the box and beheld the holy contents. As I was about to lift the Divine pen, Medusa lunged at me from behind and knocked me off my feet. This time I gave her everything I had.

All my martial arts training came into play in that moment. I was determined not to be defeated. I wouldn't allow her to steal the Divine pen, or write the final chapter for the fate of humanity. With all that I am, I fought. Then, out of nowhere my grandmother became visible and called out to Medusa. They, too, had a score to settle. I had never seen my grandmother so full of fury and anger. She believed our family was wronged by Medusa. My grandmother was going to finish her.

"You have attacked my family for the last time, Medusa!" declared my grandmother, as she flung a steel star at Medusa's throat.

It seemed my grandmother had trained in the martial arts without my knowledge, but I was relieved to see what a master she was.

Medusa caught the star. "You are a fool, Euterpe. You always were and are no match for me!" retaliated Medusa, as she threw the star back at my grandmother.

"Medusa, it is you who are the fool, for today you will be defeated for the last time," declared my grandmother as she held up her hand toward the steel star. With her ki energy, she re-directed it back to Medusa.

I was terrified and couldn't stand that my grandmother was fighting this battle. I drew my bow with another arrow, which miraculously appeared and aimed it at Medusa. Even though her back was to me, I could still hit her heart if I aimed the arrow properly and with enough energy. I drew the bow back and held my gaze on her, steady, focused, and with all of my intention. My grandmother called out an ancient chant, a formula for power, which seemed to disorient Medusa.

"Calliope, now!" my grandmother yelled to me.

Just then I released the arrow with my kiai, a piercing shout from the center of my being, which pulled in and unified all my power from the corners of the universe. I trained for many years to develop a powerful kiai, a skill that distracts an enemy and assists the execution of any technique.

At the same time, my grandmother threw a knife she had hidden in her boot with a loud kiai. Our kiais and spirits joined in the air. The arrow and the knife both traveled with the swiftness of the wind. I could hear them rushing, each intended for the heart of Medusa. Both were aimed and released with such power they never wavered from their path. They hit Medusa's heart at the same time, crushing her to the ground. Medusa yelled out, but knew she was defeated. Finally, she fell to the ground with a heavy thud that crackled like thunder.

My grandmother cautioned me not to go too close until we were sure Medusa was eternally defeated, and guided me to wait where I was. Artemis then spoke and assured us that Medusa was indeed dead. I embraced my grandmother and a flood of tears ran down my face. She, too, cried. We realized what we had just accomplished. Holding my hand, she walked me to the interior of the Temple. Then she instructed me to take hold of the Divine pen.

"It is time to fulfill your destiny, Calliope," my grandmother said as she stroked my hair. She stepped back so I could claim the pen on my own.

Reverently, I walked to the altar and gazed at the Divine pen within the marble box. It glistened and

The Circle of Olympians

was full of Light. Why I had been chosen for this monumental task I still didn't know, but I was sure I would fulfill it. I knelt before it and said a deeper prayer of thanks. I asked to be worthy of the task before me and finally dared to touch the pen. When I did, it tingled in my hand and glistened. Then I heard the Divine voice.

"Well done, Calliope. Well done. You have fulfilled your destiny and purpose in life. You will be rewarded well. Now you will write the final chapter of the ancient scroll. Do not fear, for it is I who will write the ending, using your hand. I had to know that humanity cared enough to save itself. That you succeeded proves this to be true. The final chapter will be even brighter than your vision atop the mountain on Delos. It will be more glorious than you could ever imagine. Everyone will be filled with pure love, and their hearts will be fulfilled for eternity.

"The world will be a utopia, the paradise I meant for the earth to be," said the Divine. "My greatest wish will be fulfilled and humanity will love one another as family should love family. The natural beauty of the world will be restored, the oceans will be cleansed, and the air and soil will be pure. The trees, rainforest, mountains, animals, flowers, air, crystals will return to their natural state of perfection. Humanity will never again harm these gifts of Nature. There will be no more war, no more poverty, no more disease, no more famine, and no more hatred or jealousy. All needs will be met. All that will remain will be love and beauty."

I was overcome and in awe. I knelt in humility and gratitude and sobbed a joyous cry.

"Take the pen and go complete the final chapter," instructed the Divine.

Awed, I held the Divine pen and put it into my medicine pouch. I left the Temple of Artemis, and when I saw my grandmother, I ran to her with all my heart, and collapsed in her arms. I was so happy and so relieved that she and Uncle George were all right. I almost fainted from exhaustion, both physical and emotional. But I was at peace, for I knew we were victorious over our enemy, and that I would write the final chapter. Gaea and Artemis joined us, as did Amphitrite and Eos. Each one embraced me and shared in our joy.

I hugged Uncle George desperately, for he kept his word to me. I thanked and embraced Artemis and expressed profound gratitude for the help of my dolphin friends. We rejoiced and gave thanks to God for His help and guidance in our victory. Then Medusa's body was taken away by the animals, and the temple gardens were clean.

"Well done, Calliope. I knew you would succeed," said Gaea.

"You see, Calliope, you are stronger than you think. I am pleased you now know how strong you are. There was no other way to teach you that lesson, young warrior," said Artemis as she caressed my bow.

"The Light was with you, Calliope, and it also protected your precious grandmother," said Eos, as she caressed my back.

"From the first moment, Calliope, I knew the destiny of humankind was safe in your hands. You trusted yourself and your training and relied on God, and allowed us to help you. For that you will be greatly rewarded," said Amphitrite.

"Calliope, I knew you wouldn't let us down," said Uncle George.

I thanked all of them for their help and support. I thanked Uncle George for taking care of my grandmother and for letting me know they were all right when I was most distressed. I took a deep breath, taking in everything I had just experienced.

I picked up my bow and caressed it, grateful for its protection. I could still hear Apollo's lyre and the music of the Muses. I thanked them, too, and knew what I still had to do. Apollo then appeared, followed by the Muses. It was a glorious delight to see them again and hear their music so close to my soul. I was enraptured and hoped I would remember that moment for the rest of my life. I wanted to write everything down but knew I couldn't. Instead, I would have to write everything I had seen and experienced on my soul for eternity. Everything I had ever heard about or read about Grecian antiquity was true: all the magic, all the adventure, all the myths. It was all true!

Together we celebrated in the garden before the Temple, singing, dancing, drinking nectar, and eating ambrosia. I was delirious and enraptured. While I should have been spiritually beyond it, I was happy to have delivered revenge to my archenemy and the enemy of my family. I had righted eons of wrongs and something in my soul was free.

Chapter Twenty One

༶

The Final Chapter

After we rejoiced and thanked God, we meditated and I had a glorious vision. I knew what I was to write for the final chapter. It was time to write it.

"Calliope," Apollo said, "we want to take you to Epidaurus, for healing and purification before you complete your divine task. You may already know that it is dedicated to my son, Asclepius, the god of healing and medicine. It will do your spirit good to be cleansed in that holy sanctuary," he said comfortingly.

Everyone gathered around me, as we were truly bonded by what we had gone through. Perhaps they were already bonded long ago, and I was newly initiated. Everybody looked as if they needed healing, especially my grandmother, so we gathered our things and prepared to set off for Epidaurus. I took special hold of the Divine pen, gathered my bow, and made sure I still had the amulet. Apollo gave my grandmother the ancient scroll. Artemis checked her arrows in her bag, just in case. Gaea smiled softly at the setting sun, and Eos confidently held the light for all of us to see. Amphitrite and the flying dolphins circled around us joyously, and the Muses played their music and blessed us with their presence.

Magically, we were on the outskirts of the sanctuary of Epidaurus. I instantly felt a release deep within my being. The atmosphere smelled cleaner than air I had ever smelled, and the energy was pure. I understood why the ancients journeyed to Epidaurus for healing treatments and purification. How lucky I was to experience it for myself. Together we walked in silent meditation deep into the woods of the sanctuary, each one looking for their own sacred spot to sleep for healing.

First Gaea found her perfect place, followed by Artemis, Eos, and then Amphitrite. The Muses followed Apollo and rested near him, as he put his lyre down and laid down to rest. My grandmother instructed me to choose a place, using my center and instinct. She said I would know when I found the right place. We walked a bit together. I then felt something deep within my soul stir and knew I found my healing, resting place. I put my bow and belongings down and asked my grandmother to stay near me. She promised she would. She invited Uncle George to rest near us as well. When we were all properly situated, all of us slept for what felt like years.

I had spectacular dreams in Epidauras. I saw worlds and new cities not yet known to humankind. Secrets were revealed to me about healing. I was to take back some of those secrets with me when I returned to California. My dreams told me I was supposed to use the healing I was learning about in Epidaurus to help others. The healing secrets I was learning would also find their way into my writing, which I hoped would help heal others.

Once again, I didn't want to leave this paradise, but knew I was there to prepare for writing the final chapter of the ancient scroll. I tried to put the stress of that duty out of my mind while I was at Epidaurus to receive the full benefit of the healing. I quieted my mind with my breath and entered a deeper dream state.

In my dream, my grandmother spoke to me. She told me my journey was almost complete, but there were two more places I had to visit before my work was done. I couldn't hear the names of the places I was to visit, but then heard the Voice of God guide me. He told me He would speak to me, and write the final chapter of the ancient scroll through my hand, using the Divine pen. Then I began to wake up.

Gaea told me, "It is time for us to go. There is a divine timing to things, and we don't want to miss it or play with it. Gather your things and do not forget the Divine pen."

Eos smiled gently, waking me easily from my deep slumber. Artemis gathered her bow and arrows and gave me some extra arrows for safekeeping. Apollo stood before us and gathered the Muses around him. Amphitrite, the flying dolphins, Uncle George, and my grandmother gathered around me and helped me gather my things. They made sure I had everything I needed, including the amulet. All had rested well in Epidaurus, and all had been refreshed, renewed, and healed. I would never forget it, and vowed to return one day.

I wasn't sure where we were going but had learned to trust the care I was in. Gaea instructed us to close our eyes, breathe deeply, and focus on the Divine Light. Together we journeyed to another dimension of consciousness. I was absorbed by the Light and felt transported to an island with a very potent energy.

Gaea then instructed us to open our eyes, and we were on the island of Patmos, the place where Saint John received and wrote Revelations. It was mystical and beautiful in a way I had never felt before. In silence, and following Gaea, we walked to a secret cave, hidden deep within the mountains. She parted some bushes to reveal a doorway and guided me to enter.

"Calliope, this is where you will write the final chapter of the ancient and sacred scroll," Gaea said to

The Circle of Olympians

me. "You must do this alone, but you are safe now. We will guard the entryway to this sacred cave. You must go now for it is the proper celestial time for you to complete your great assignment."

I braced myself, hugged each one and thanked them for their wisdom, love, support, and teachings. I breathed deeply, centered myself, and took everything I had carried and fought to own with me into the cave. It was frightening at first because it was so dark, but it wasn't negative. I felt as if I was going into the womb of the earth, the womb of the universe. The air was moist and I felt others had walked this path before me.

The path I walked upon was dirt but the walls glistened. Then I heard a drop of water and wondered where I was going. The Voice guided me forward and with great faith, I put one foot in front of the other. I perceived a light, faint at first, but then luminous and blue gold. I was so eager and excited, my pace quickened until I arrived at an underwater cave and sanctuary.

There was a little beach and a small fire burned, seemingly awaiting me. I was on sacred ground and proceeded with reverence. Carefully and slowly I put my things down, knelt by the sacred fire, and said a prayer to God offering my thanks and devotion. I felt led to purify myself in the aqua blue water. I immersed myself in it, preparing for the writing I was about receive.

When I felt the time was right, I got out of the water, and dried myself by the heat of the flames. Then, hands shaking, I carefully took out the ancient scroll and the Divine pen. I made sure I held the amulet in my hand to connect to its energy. I centered myself and meditated. I then heard the Voice.

The Voice guided me in the secret ways of using the Divine pen, how to write upon the ancient scroll, and how to keep the stream of consciousness flowing so that I received the information in an uninterrupted flow. The pen moved and the final chapter wrote itself. I was a servant of this work, and was filled with awe and gratitude that I had been chosen for this magnificent work. I was grateful I had trained hard, learned my lessons well, passed my tests, and was victorious over Medusa.

The writing went on for hours and days, and by the time I finished I was exhausted beyond anything I had ever felt in my life. I was delirious with joy as I knew humanity was now safe, and would create a Heaven on earth and live a joyous life they would help create. The idyllic vision I had earlier prevailed over the apocalyptic one I dreaded. For that I was grateful. The final chapter had been written exactly as my vision foretold. My soul was finally unburdened of the weight of the world.

The Voice guided me to wash and purify myself once again in the aqua blue water, and I blissfully did so. The weight of my life left me under the water. I felt refreshed and joyous. I was so happy that I fulfilled my destiny, and that the Light was once again victorious. That I had played a small part in service to that victory was my greatest joy.

The Voice led me to gather my things and leave the cave, as my work was completed. It was time for me to return to my life in California. Slowly, I walked out of the cave in a state of awe. True to their word, when I walked out of the cave, everyone was there guarding the entryway to the cave and my life. They were ecstatic when I walked out for they knew it meant I had finished writing the final chapter of the ancient scroll and that I had fulfilled my destiny.

My grandmother embraced me, as did Uncle George. Eos, Artemis, Gaea, Amphitrite, Apollo, and the Muses did the same. The dolphins flew overhead joyously and the stars flew across the sky in celebration. We celebrated into the hours of dawn, and gave thanks to God for His love and guidance.

"I knew you would do it, Calliope," my grandmother beamed. "This is what you were born to do. I am very proud of you. You must keep this secret from everyone, except from your mother. You have done well and now it is time to give thanks, celebrate, and gather the spiritual rewards you earned. There is just one more place we need to visit, Calliope. We must go to Sounion, the sanctuary of Poseidon, to honor your paternal grandmother, for she also helped you without your knowledge."

"Yes, grandmother. That sounds wonderful. I would love to visit with Yia Yia again. I felt her spirit with me along this journey," I replied.

Near Cape Sounion in Greece was where my Yia Yia was born. Yia Yia was Greek for grandmother, and she and I were always close. I visited there soon after my Yia Yia had passed over, and took a remarkable photograph. I was climbing up the mountain toward the Temple of Poseidon when a voice told me, "Turn around and take the photograph." I did and when the film was developed, I could see an angel with wings and outstretched arms plainly visible. I love that photograph!

Greece, as life that summer, was an open treasure chest. It was difficult to choose which piece to select and tenderly hold in my hand. But that was Greece's beauty and her secret. I learned that all of life was a treasure chest if I knew how to see it, for perhaps the treasure is best seen with eyes closed and the soul open. Such was Greece . . . such was Sounion.

Once more, Gaea led us in prayer and meditation that transported us to another place, another dimension, and another sacred place in Greece.

Chapter Twenty Two

⟲

Yia Yia

The sun shone more brightly than I had ever seen it shine anywhere else. As soon as I set foot upon the ground of the Temple of Poseidon, I felt my Yia Yia's spirit. She always knew I was the dreamer, and she guarded and nurtured this sacred skill within me.

My Grandmother Euterpe and the Olympians encouraged me to walk up the temple hill. I was filled with profound love and peace with each step. I was led to the center of the Temple and there she was, my Yia Yia, who had passed over long ago.

"My precious granddaughter," she exclaimed. "It has been a long time since we have seen one another, but I have watched you all these years. Calliope, I have spoken to you in the wind, in the bloom of the same flowers you always gave me, and in the Greek foods you cook. I have visited your dreams to let you know I was with you, especially during the dark times in your life. I have always loved you and have never stopped guarding you.

"I am overjoyed that you fulfilled your destiny and saved humanity," Yia Yia continued, "for now all will rejoice in eternal life and joy. All suffering will cease and there will be no more tears. Your heart and soul served you well. No matter what you suffered in life, or who betrayed you or abused you, you never stopped loving, and that is what is most important.

The Circle of Olympians

You will be rewarded for this, my dear. I am very proud of you.

As she spoke I was wrapped around her, basking in her love and energy. I couldn't believe I was with her again. My heart was full and I felt I was finally home. So many of our loved ones had passed over the years, and as each one left, they took a part of my heart with them. Being with Yia Yia again, and knowing that all my loved ones were still with me even if I wasn't always aware of them, comforted me. My soul was filled with such love and peace that for the first time in a long time, I felt whole. My suffering was lifted from my heart forever.

Fulfilling my destiny was difficult because so much interfered with hearing my inner voice, the Voice of God. I was grateful for my Aikido training, for it taught me the path to follow to find myself and fulfill my destiny. I was grateful to the Olympians who had risked so much to train me, and for protecting me all along the way.

I was filled with gratitude for my grandmother and Uncle George who took such good care of me, and loved and supported me throughout my magnificent journey. They were powerful beings I was humbled to be related to. And I was grateful for my mother, my guardian angel and warrior of faith, who taught me so much about belief, especially when there was no reason to believe. She would find it difficult to believe what danger I was in that summer. But I knew she would believe every word I shared with her, as she always believed in me, especially when I did not.

I appreciated everything that happened in my life that had brought me to that moment, for all of it prepared me to fulfill a magnificent destiny. And most importantly I was grateful to God, who loved and supported me, communicated with me, guided me, and was loyal to me even when I failed Him through my doubt, fear, and grief. It was all magnificent, and I vowed I would remember all of it forever.

"Calliope," Yia Yia said, "you can return here anytime you wish, and can even visit in spirit, without physically being here. Remember this, for you will need to touch this place and its spiritual energy, and feel this moment again. You will need to connect with this energy often, for you may feel far away from it you once you return to California. Here, keep this with you always," she said as she gave me a special piece of sky blue aragonite. It looked like a piece of the ocean, found only in Sounion in an underwater cave.

"Thank you, Yia Yia," I said as I excitedly welcomed the stone into my medicine pouch. "I am grateful I will be able to return here any time. I know part of me will never leave here. My heart will always be with you, Yia Yia, and I'm so happy to be with you now," I said through tears of joy.

Then my Grandmother Euterpe, Uncle George, Gaea, Artemis, Amphitrite, Eos, Apollo, and the Muses joined us in the Temple. The dolphins flew around us, in and out of the temple columns, and we gave thanks to God. The emotion and energy was pure white Light. It filled us completely. I felt glorious!

Chapter Twenty Three

◈

Goodbyes

Apollo told me it was time to return the Divine pen to its rightful place in the Temple of Artemis on the island of Delos. I had to replace it as only the hand that removed it from the marble box could return it. The way we had traveled thus far that summer is how we returned to Delos. I reverently walked into the Temple of Artemis and safely returned the Divine pen to its sacred resting place. I put the marble lid back on the box, said a prayer of thanks, and walked out of the Temple in awe and wonderment.

"Well done, Calliope. Well done. It is time for me to go home now, but we will meet again, perhaps in your dreams, perhaps on another divine mission," said Apollo. "Know that you have done well. You learned your lessons and immersed yourself in your training, and you brought about a new idyllic age for humanity. Never forget us or this experience, but be careful with whom you share it. There will be a time of transition for humanity to enter into the new time. You must guard yourself well during this time. Never forget that we are with you," said Apollo as he said goodbye to me and left with the Muses.

I thanked him for everything he had done for me, and cried as we said goodbye. I thanked the Muses for their beauty, their music, and their serenity. I desperately hoped I would see or hear them again.

Then my grandmother, Gaea, Artemis, Eos, Amphitrite, and Uncle George gathered around me, preparing to journey to the Sacred Grove for one more visit, before I returned to Ithaca and finally back to California. I felt a peace I had never known before as these goddesses and Olympians surrounded me. I would never be able to thank them for what they had taught me and done for me. All that I could do from that moment on was to emulate them to the best of my ability.

At that moment, under Gaea's guidance, we were transported to the Sacred Grove for one more celebration. I loved the Grove and never wanted to leave. If there was a paradise on earth, surely that was it. We entered the temple gardens and purified ourselves in the baths once more. We prayed and meditated, gave thanks to God, and left an offering of crystals. We sang and laughed and celebrated for hours beside the sacred flame. The dolphins flew overhead, and added their love and healing. Eos provided the luminous dawn. I took it all into my soul. Afterward, we slept for what felt like days. When I awoke, Artemis, Eos, and Amphitrite were by my side.

"Calliope, it is time for us to go," said Artemis. "You will be safe now, but remember your training and keep your bow and arrows in a safe, hidden place. Your journey home will be smooth, but we will watch over you until you are safely in California. Remember what Apollo told you, that we will always be with you and that you can always join us in spirit. We will meet again, how and where I am not sure, but we will meet again," Artemis said as she embraced me powerfully.

"Artemis, you have taught me so much. You taught me about power, strength, focus, and how to believe in myself. I never would have fulfilled my destiny without your help and guidance. You are the warrior of all warriors and I will train the rest of my life to be like you," I said as I held her tightly.

The Circle of Olympians

"Whenever you wish to be with me, look up to the stars, let your vision become soft, and you will see me and feel me. Remember this always," Artemis said as she sprinkled some stardust into the palm of my hand. "Keep this in your medicine pouch and I will always be near."

I clasped my hand around the precious stardust and thanked her with tears streaming down my face. Gently I opened my medicine pouch and poured the stardust inside it.

Eos gently stroked my back and said, "Calliope, I too will always be with you. Every morning when you arise, know that I am there. Even when nighttime falls, I am still there, but am only lighting the day for another part of the world. Knowing this will strengthen your faith. Knowing that the Light is there, even when you cannot see it, is the supreme testament of faith. Call on me anytime you need your path to be lit, or need to know whether or not you are on your path, and I will light the way. I am always with you. Keep this in your medicine pouch as a reminder of me," Eos said as she handed me a small, brilliantly lit crystal.

"Thank you, Eos. I promise to remember your teaching and to call upon you when I need your Light to illuminate my path and my world," I said as I humbly took the crystal and placed it in my medicine pouch.

Then Amphitrite comforted me as she prepared to say goodbye. "You have done well, Calliope. Remember us," she said as she waved her arm towards our dolphin friends, "and remember the lessons of the sea Poseidon taught you. Never forget the ocean is your friend, and all the creatures that dwell within her waters," Amphitrite said as she gave me another shell to keep in my medicine bag.

"Hold this close to your heart, and to your ear whenever you want to feel close to us. You will always be able to breathe underwater and visit Poseidon's temple whenever you wish. Look for me in the blue depths and I will never be far. I, too, will always be with you and watch over you for the rest of your life," Amphitrite said.

"I will never forget you, Amphitrite, nor the lessons you and our dolphin friends and Poseidon taught me in the great blue depths," I said as I humbly took the precious shell and added it to my sacred possessions within my medicine pouch.

As I added each precious piece into my medicine pouch, more energy filled my body and spirit. I was blessed with great gifts and experiences. I prayed to be worthy of keeping them deep within my heart.

Amphitrite hugged me goodbye as she, Eos, and Artemis left the Sacred Grove. Gaea and my grandmother and Uncle George remained, and I knew it was time for us to go, too. Uncle George gathered his and my grandmother's things, and Gaea held my hands and said a final prayer as we prepared to leave. Then I gathered my things, and we were ready to leave.

Uncle George escorted us back to Gaea's cave. He told my grandmother he would meet us back at their house in Ithaca. He wanted to make sure everything was secure, and that it would be safe for us to return. Gaea, my grandmother, and I shared some final precious moments together in Gaea's cave. We sat in prayer and gave thanks for what felt like hours. The images of the Olympians that took form on the walls of the cave had disappeared, as their mission was accomplished.

"Grandmother, what happens to me now? What do I do now? How can I return to my life in California after such an extraordinary adventure and summer?" I asked.

My grandmother centered herself and looked at Gaea. She took a deep breath and revealed a final

The Circle of Olympians

secret. I saw blue smoke form around her feet and the air was suddenly filled with an intoxicating aroma.

"Calliope," my grandmother said, "I am the great priestess of Delphi. Thousands of years ago Apollo gave me the gift of prophecy. I have guided thousands of pilgrims since that time. I can see far into the future. This has been a great weight for me to carry all these years. That you can now join me in this responsibility will take a great burden off my shoulders. What I am about to reveal to you is sacred and meant for your ears only. You must swear to keep what I am about to tell you secret," my grandmother commanded.

Once again, I almost fainted because of what my grandmother just shared with me. I thought I had fulfilled my destiny and the work God intended for me. Now I suddenly felt completely overwhelmed again and was unsure of what my grandmother was telling me. By now, I learned that I couldn't escape or refuse my destiny, no matter how I felt, so I had to swear the oath my grandmother asked of me.

"Yes, grandmother, I swear to guard your secret," I vowed.

"When you were very young, you had the gift of seership. I knew it the first time I held you in my arms as a baby. Your mother also knew this but we had to protect you and your destiny, and therefore didn't develop your abilities when you were a child. However, your abilities developed on their own. Now it is time to develop them to their highest level. Don't think of this as daunting, but as a way of helping those around you.

"Perhaps one day, when I am too tired to continue, you might become the oracle at Delphi," my grandmother continued. "But do this only if you want to. Your decision will be many years ahead, so there is time for you to contemplate this. In the meantime, I want you to meditate regularly and for longer periods of time. I will teach you new techniques to practice. You will expand your abilities and see visions for the world. Always use your talents to serve God and you will always be protected and given greater spiritual gifts," my grandmother told me.

She taught me a new meditation technique and we practiced together for a long time. She gave me a small crystal to anchor the experience and keep with me always, which I added to my medicine bag. Gaea gave me a bit of earth for my pouch to remind me of the energy of her sacred cave. Then it was time for my grandmother and I to go home.

"Gaea, how can I say goodbye to you?" I said through many tears.

"Don't worry, Calliope. I will always be with you. Don't you know that by now? You can visit me anytime you wish, but you will be busier than you think in California. There is one more Olympian who will come into your life, a great love, but I cannot tell you more than that. I know this has been much for you to endure, but you have done admirably. Never forget who you are, where you came from, your lineage, and what your destiny is. Claim your fortune and take your place beside the Olympians for you earned it well. Remember, I am always with you," Gaea said as she gave me a final kiss on the forehead and an embrace.

I thanked her for everything and could barely talk. I held her with my entire being and sobbed as we left her sanctuary. My grandmother shared a private moment with her sister and promised to return soon. There was still a lot of work for the two of them to do. They would accomplish it victoriously.

Chapter Twenty Four

Return to Ithaca

My grandmother held me with all her strength as we walked out of the earth womb and into the daylight of Ithaca. She used her walking stick again for the first time since our journey began that summer, which seemed to fill her with much needed energy. I looked at her with a question in my eye.

My grandmother knew my thoughts, and said with a mischievous smile, "Next summer, I will teach you how to use this!"

I was in a daze. My grandmother held my arm as we walked back to her house by the same path we had walked to enter Gaea's cave. My grandmother knew I was overwhelmed, and comforted me with her love. I took each step mindfully and tried to sort through everything I had experienced.

Finally we were home, and Uncle George prepared a full dinner for us. The house smelled as delicious as it always did. It embraced us with its warmth and aromas. I hugged Uncle George and thanked him for cooking such a wonderful meal. I put my things down in my room. My grandmother looked tired, too, as she put her things down. She returned her copy of the ancient scroll to her secret cupboard.

Then we sat down together, said a prayer, and enjoyed the best meal I ever had in my life. I thanked them both, kissed them goodnight, and went to bed early. The icon in my room still glowed, as if it still had secrets to tell me, but I was too tired to meditate on it. I slept deeply and for many hours. When I arose, I prayed and meditated as my grandmother had instructed me.

Chapter Twenty Five

The Artifacts of Athens

The rest of my summer days I spent with my grandmother and Uncle George, enjoying the simple pleasures of Greek island life. I cherished those days and didn't want them to end. But before long, the summer did come to an end. It was time for me to return to California to resume my life. I had no idea how I would carry on in California after such a miraculous summer in Greece, but it was time for me to go. It was just a matter of time before I would return to Greece next summer, and to what adventure, I wasn't sure. My grandmother and Uncle George planned to visit us in California for Christmas, so it wouldn't be too long before I would see them again.

The day I was ready to leave I packed my things, and held my grandmother for as long as I could. Our bond had grown even deeper. I would always carry a part of her deep within my soul. We were part of each other, and that part grew deeper that summer. My love for Uncle George also deepened. I was too overwhelmed to say goodbye to either one of them. I couldn't speak the words.

They walked me down to the harbor and waited with me for my boat. It eventually came. We embraced a final time and I promised I would call as soon as I got home. We reminded each other we would see one another very soon, and my grandmother promised she would try to learn "the e-mail." As I turned to leave, my grandmother stopped me. She touched my arm, and without saying a word, handed me the amulet.

"No, I can't," I protested.

"I want you to have this. It is your turn to be its keeper. And it will protect you whenever you need to be invisible. Keep it with you always. Promise!"

I nodded my head in agreement and clutched the amulet. I quickly put it around my neck again, and spoke the ancient chant that allowed me to be visible while wearing the amulet. This was such an honor. I then tearfully left my grandmother after one last long look and hug, and boarded with my sacred treasures in my medicine pouch and in my bags.

Sadly, I walked up the ramp of the boat, and up a few flights of stairs to get to the deck. I looked down at the dock for my grandmother and Uncle George. But something caught my eye off in the distance. I looked toward the horizon and suddenly recognized it.

Mount Olympus rose heavenward in the distant mist. I stared at it and slowly, magically I saw them . . . the ancient Olympians. Even in the distance they looked fierce. But I wasn't afraid. They had become my teachers, my mentors, and my friends. I couldn't know if they saw me but I waved at them. Then I looked back at my grandmother and Uncle George and waved one last time from the deck of the boat. We slowly pulled out of the harbor, and when I could no longer see them, I went below, took my seat, and began to write in my journal.

I wanted to remember everything, yet couldn't break the vow I made to keep everything I learned sacred. As I started to write a code came to mind, from where I don't know. Only I would understand it. I made some notes in code, of what I experienced and felt that summer in Greece. I couldn't trust myself to

The Circle of Olympians

remember everything, and wanted to have a record of it to refer to. When I wanted to write about the most sacred moments, my hand stopped. I knew that even in code some of it was too sacred to write about.

I made some drawings in the margins of my journal, to further remind me of the magic I had experienced. The more I wrote, the more my mind was taken off how much I already missed my grandmother and Uncle George. Writing was always a dear friend to me, and it once again comforted me in a time of great need. While I felt victorious and joyous for fulfilling my life's work, I was exhausted and ready to return to California, and to my own home and bed.

The rest of the boat ride went smoothly, and I slept for an hour or so. When we arrived in Piraeus, I waited. I didn't want to get pushed and shoved as I was trying to remain in the sacred space I had spent the summer in. After most of the passengers left, I gathered my bags and walked off the boat into the frenzied port, looking for a taxi to take me into Athens for a few days.

I stayed with a cousin of my mom's, Voula. I didn't feel like talking too much when I first arrived at her house, even though I loved her and her family dearly. So much happened over the summer. I had to take time to digest all of it and make it part of my being and the rest of my life. Voula cooked a fantastic welcoming dinner for me, and showed me to an immaculate guest room. I gave her a beautiful linen tablecloth, handmade in Ithaca. She said she would always think of me whenever she used it.

I was exhausted but couldn't sleep and wrote more coded notes in my journal. Although I only had a few days in Athens, I wanted to go to the National Archeological Museum and the Byzantine Museum to study a few artifacts.

The next day I woke up early and was still tired. Voula had strong coffee brewed for me and asked if I wanted company to the museums. Although I wanted to go alone I couldn't be rude, especially since she was my hostess, so she joined me. We decided to walk to the National Museum as it was too early for the sidewalks to be crowded. I could feel the ancient spirits still dwelling in the city. Voula didn't say too much, but it was nice to have her company, even though I initially wanted to be alone.

When we finally arrived, the doors of the museum had just opened. I was anxious to get inside. I rushed to the statues and looked closely at all of them, especially the bronze charioteer. I studied all the ancient artifacts, and was amazed by the ingenuity of the ancients. The museum even showcased a replica of Artemis' bow and Apollo's lyre, which mesmerized me. I stood before them in awe. I had seen the real artifacts, and knew I couldn't react in any way that would reveal this. Voula could tell something was on my mind, but I guarded the secrets well for I made a solemn vow I intended to keep.

We walked into another room that housed the artifacts from Delos. I was suddenly overcome with missing the island I grew so attached to. There was a re-creation of the sacred temple, which I knew housed the Divine pen. Most of it looked familiar, but some of it was incorrect. I was delighted to look at my cherished places and sacred spots many still did not know about.

We looked at some murals from the Mycenaean era, including paintings of flying dolphins. They winked at me as I studied their form, and I was delighted by my connection with them. I saw paintings of Amphitrite, and of Eos and Gaea, my beloved friends and teachers. There was a statue of Apollo, a painting of the Muses, jewelry, and little amulets and tools the ancients had used long ago. They were letting me know they were

The Circle of Olympians

with me in the museum. I felt ecstatic and deeply comforted.

I touched my amulet, which my grandmother insisted I take with me, hidden within my medicine pouch. I made sure all my sacred objects were there too, while trying not to call attention to myself. All of it had really happened, I thought to myself. Everything I experienced was real. I was so blessed to have received this great gift. I wondered what I would leave behind for others to look at and learn from when it was my time to leave this life. Perhaps my journal would one day be housed in a special case, in a special museum, with experts trying to break the code?

Voula and I exhausted ourselves spending the entire morning in the museum. We went for lunch and sauntered off to the smaller, more intimate Byzantine museum, which housed precious religious artifacts. I loved that museum. I felt as if I were in an empty church, which always made me feel closest to God. Silently we walked through the museum, and I studied every sacred object displayed. My entire walk through that museum was a prayer and a walking meditation.

Walking through the museums helped me put that entire summer into perspective. I had to seal my experiences and new knowledge within my being. Visiting the museums and seeing the artifacts helped anchor my miraculous experiences within my soul. The day had been full. It was time to go home.

Chapter Twenty Six

Return to California

    I napped a bit in the afternoon, and woke up for a late supper and visiting other relatives in Athens before getting ready to return to California. I called my grandmother in Ithaca because I missed her too much already, and then went to bed early. The next day, I woke up early and showered to prepare myself for the long journey back to California. I called my mom to let her know my flight time and number, told her I loved her, and that I was excited to see her as I missed her terribly. She told me she loved me, too, and that she would be waiting for me at the airport.

    I thanked Voula for everything, and told her to come to California whenever she wanted. She promised to visit soon, perhaps for Christmas. I was happy to hear that, and was then ready to go. Voula's son George offered to drive us to the airport. We rode in the early morning, watching the sunrise, and quickly arrived at the airport. I traveled light and didn't have any bags to check, nor did I want to chance losing any of my precious belongings.

    I waited on line to check in, and once I was settled Voula kissed me and hugged me one final time. She waved goodbye as I went through security and headed for the gate. I felt re-birthed at that moment. I knew I had crossed some sort of threshold. At the gate, I sat

The Circle of Olympians

down, placed my bags beside me and waited to board my flight. After an hour or so, they finally called us to board the plane. I took my seat and put my bag carefully beneath the seat in front of me to keep an eye on it at all times. I felt the amulet in my medicine pouch. I was overwhelmed that my grandmother had entrusted this magnificent family treasure to me.

I buckled myself in my seat and slept for most of the flight home. I didn't eat any of the food, nor did I talk to anyone. I was still somewhere else spiritually, and wanted to remain there as long as I possibly could.

At last, the twelve-hour flight finally landed in San Francisco. I was anxious to see my mom. I missed her and wanted to share everything with her. But how could I share everything with her while keeping my sacred vow?

All of the passengers were waking up from the long flight, gathering their scattered things, bags, blankets, pillows, kids, coats, and slowly making their way off the plane. I waited for most people to get off. I wasn't in a hurry. Slowly, I walked out of the plane, and into the airport terminal. Mom would have usually been waiting at the gate, but since security had changed, I had to wait just a few more moments to see her inside the terminal.

Anxious to see her, I quickened my pace even though I was lugging bags and was exhausted on all levels. Faintly at first, but then clearly, I saw her beautiful smile and waving arms. My mom was there for me as she always was, thrilled to see me. As we got closer to one another, we both lit up, and were joyous to be together again. If there are past lives, my mom and I have shared many of them. Finally I was in her arms, embraced in her eternal love and safety. No one would ever love me as much or as unconditionally as my mother, and I was grateful she was my mom. God truly blessed me when he made her my mother.

She looked at me as she held my face in her hands and told me how happy she was to see me, and how much she had missed me. I told her I loved her too, that there was so much I had to tell her, and that she would never believe what I had gone through that summer. She knew me well, and knew that I needed to go home and sleep in my own bed.

We drove home easily and caught up with one another, and some of the family gossip. I wanted to tell her everything, but wasn't sure how much I could reveal. I told her I promised to call grandmother when I got home, and mom said she talked to grandma earlier that day. They loved me very much, my mom said, and had a delightful time with me over the summer. Mom was pretty sure grandmother and Uncle George would visit us for Christmas, but they were a little tired. If mom only knew!

We got home before it was dark and it felt strange yet good to be home. So much had happened since I left earlier that summer. My life had completely changed. I wasn't sure I would ever fit into my old life again. How would I acclimate my new abilities and adventures, and my true spiritual destiny with the mundane life I had been living? I had a lot of praying and meditating to do. I had to keep my promise to my grandmother to meditate regularly using the new techniques she taught me.

As I entered our home, I felt a strange spirit I hadn't felt before. It didn't frighten me, but comforted me and felt familiar. Maybe the Olympians were watching over me after all? Mom had everything so nice in the house. She had set beautiful pink roses in my room to welcome me. It felt good to be home as I plumped myself onto my bed. Nothing felt as warm and embracing as one's own bed. I breathed deeply and settled myself. Traveling took a great toll on my system even though I loved it. It always took me a day

The Circle of Olympians

or two to pull myself together after a long flight and different time zones and countries.

Mom cooked something special and its aromas wafted up to my room, calling me to dinner even though I was too tired to eat. My godmother, or Nouna in Greek, was on her way over as she missed me too, and couldn't wait to see me. She was my mother's sister and they were very close. I wondered if they knew who Euterpe, their mother, really was? If my Nouna was on her way, I had to stay awake for dinner. I mustered up some energy as I changed into my pajamas and walked downstairs to the kitchen.

Chapter Twenty Seven

୬୨

Family Reunion

The doorbell rang and my Nouna jumped through the doorway and quickly embraced me. Mom was happy to see her too, and we held each other in a family hug. She kissed me hello and was so happy to see me. I felt so loved by her and my mom, and knew I was very blessed.

Before I left for the summer I felt so depressed, hopeless, and discouraged about my life. I forgot what was important because I was buried in my grief. The summer taught me to be grateful for what I had left in my life, and to carry on with what I still had. I learned I could still shine, even if I felt all of life and light had left me.

I loved my mom and Nouna with all my heart. That summer, my life had been filled with such love and camaraderie, I felt embraced no matter where I went. I successfully internalized that love and support and wanted to share it with others. I couldn't wait to go back to Aikido and my family at the dojo. There, too, I had been gifted with a heroine teacher and exceptional students to train with, who had become my extended family over the years. What they taught me and prepared me for, they would never know, but I would be eternally grateful to them for the training.

The Circle of Olympians

Mom and I and my Nouna talked about the summer. I filled them in on the family in Greece, and what everyone was doing. They told me what happened in California that summer, and what they did together. I was glad they had one another as they were good company for each other. They looked at me expecting me to share something with them, but I wasn't sure what I could reveal, or how much, if anything, they knew.

Mom asked me a few questions about what grandmother and I did, and if she was different this summer. I suspected mom knew something but couldn't be sure how much she or my Nouna knew. Then my mom stepped out of the kitchen and went to her bedroom. She unlocked the safe that was hidden behind a secret wall and came out with a small, wooden, ancient chest. I didn't know what to expect when she came back to the kitchen. I looked at her, and then at my Nouna.

"Mom, what is that?" I asked. "I've never seen it before."

"This box was given to me a long time ago, when I was a little girl. I used to play with it all the time, pretending I was a princess, and this was my treasure chest," my mom said.

"I remember that. You used to drive me crazy with that chest!" laughed my Nouna.

I laughed too and wanted to touch it. It had an energy, which was somehow familiar to me. My mom unlocked and opened it. Inside were many treasures I couldn't believe had been in our house all this time! There were precious and priceless gems, Greek antiquities, gold coins, and an ancient scroll! I just about passed out! So did my Nouna! I guess she hadn't seen the contents of the box in a while, but my mom was busy over the years collecting the precious and sacred contents.

"Calliope," my mother said, "the contents of this box must remain secret. You mustn't tell anyone about what I have revealed to you. If anyone ever finds out we have these things, we will no longer be safe," my mother cautioned.

"Mom, don't worry about that anymore. I took care of things this summer. There is so much I have to tell you, but I'm not sure what I'm supposed to keep secret, and what I'm allowed to reveal," I said.

Then my mother said, "I'll be right back," as she left the kitchen again.

When she returned, I almost fell off my seat, for in her hands she held Artemis' bow and arrows!

Chapter Twenty Eight

Joyous Revelation

"Mom, what are you trying to tell me? Why do you have Artemis' bow and arrows?" I asked, in awe.

As soon as I finished asking my question, it dawned on me who my mother really was. No wonder she was such a warrior all her life! And I thought she wouldn't be able to handle the truth of what I had gone through that summer! I laughed but was in shock. As I realized who she was, I was thrilled. Artemis said she would keep an eye on me, and to now know she was my mother was fabulous!

"Calliope, my darling goddaughter, I, too have a secret to reveal to you," my Nouna said as she stood up, with a twinkle in her eye.

For the first time in my life, as I looked at my Nouna, I saw an incredible aura of light around her. It cast a warm glow in the kitchen and as she smiled, her light and aura grew brighter. I looked at my mother and she smiled at me and at my Nouna.

"Nouna, you are the dawn, you are Eos!" I exclaimed as I realized who she was.

"Yes, darling, I am she!" she confirmed as she smiled at me. "I also promised to be with you always, but I know it's a surprise for you to realize just how close we would be. You are very precious to us, and we couldn't chance telling you any earlier in your life who we really were," my Nouna said as she caressed my face.

I hid my face in her neck and my mom caressed my back.

"Calliope, my beautiful golden girl, I know it is a lot for you to absorb, but don't you feel better knowing you can share everything with us, as we were there with you this summer? Think of how isolated you would have felt if you couldn't share anything with us. Your Nouna and I also made vows this summer, and vows long ago that we have kept through your victory. This is a night for us to cherish, to celebrate with one another, and to give thanks to God," my mother said. "Calliope," she continued, "I know how tired you are, sweetie, but we should go to church to light a candle and get a blessing from Father Elias."

"OK, mom. You're right. We have a lot to be grateful for. I'll be ready in a few minutes. Just let me eat something," I said.

"Of course, sweetie," my mom said as she filled my plate with her soul-filling food.

We said a prayer and ate together. Nothing filled my heart as much as eating a beautifully home cooked meal with family that I loved so much. When I finished eating, I went up to my room, and knelt to say a private prayer. I changed into comfortable but formal clothes, and was ready.

We got into our car and drove to church. We entered the vestibule, made an offering, lit candles, said prayers, and kissed the icons. There was a special service that night, and it felt good and safe to be in my home church with the familiar incense and hypnotic chants.

Father Elias saw us and smiled, as he flawlessly led the service. He was a brilliant priest and scholar, and was very charismatic. He was blessed with so many gifts, spoke many languages, and played many instruments. His most important gift was that he made everyone who entered his church feel welcomed.

The Circle of Olympians

As I listened to the choir, I thought I heard the strain of music the Muses had played. Was it possible they were here too? I hoped so as I looked at the choir for clues of my new friends. I heard them and felt their spirits, and thought I saw their faces within the choir. I no longer questioned the miraculous, but accepted it as part of everyday life.

While the service continued, my mother whispered in my ear, "Maybe next summer, we can all go to Greece. There is an ancient Mystery School I would like to take you to," she said with a mischievous grin.

I smiled at her, wondering what could possibly happen next summer in Greece. Another Mystery School! Unbelievable!

As the church service ended, and we went up for blessed bread, I kissed Father Elias' hand and received the bread and his blessing, as all parishioners did. He welcomed me home with his healing touch. Just being in his presence made me feel safe. I noticed there was a new instrument by the church organ, and I asked him about it.

"Oh, that's a lyre someone just sent me from Greece. I haven't a clue how to play it but I thought I would give it a try for the Christmas pageant this year," Father Elias said. "I'm glad you're home, Calliope. We have much to talk about. Come by after church on Sunday and we will have a nice talk," he said as he patted my hand.

Looking at the lyre, I realized Father Elias was Apollo! I couldn't believe it. Now, I really needed to go home and go to bed or watch some mindless television.

After saying hello to some friends, Mom and I and my Nouna walked to our car and drove home. My Nouna spent the night with us, and for this I was relieved. I kissed my mom and Nouna goodnight, and they held me close. We told each other how much we loved one another. I called my grandmother, Euterpe, to tell her and Uncle George that I had arrived home safely and that I would call again over the weekend to talk more. I watched some television, and finally went up to my room to go to bed.

I said my evening prayers holding my amulet, and placed my medicine pouch in front of my icon of Jesus. I prayed to Him and thanked Him for everything He had done for me. I thanked God for giving me such wonderful elders: my mother, my grandmother, my godmother, my Uncle George, and the guidance and protection of the Olympians. I thanked Him for carrying me home safely, and for not leaving me alone with all my memories and experiences. I was so grateful I could share everything with my mother and godmother, and was in awe of God's brilliance. Truly He was the Genius of the Universe.

As I sat in meditation for a brief time, I had another vision: I saw the world completely at peace, held in a blue silence that seemed to be the womb of the universe. It was a brief vision, but that night I knew that all was well in the world.

I went to bed, tucked the covers delightedly over my shoulders and closed my eyes, hoping I would dream of the Sacred Grove.

The End . . . For now

If you would like to contact Sonya Haramis, M.Ed., or order additional books, please visit:
www.peaceofthedreamer.com

Blessings, Love, and Light!